For more than forty years,
Yearling has been the leading name
in classic and award-winning literature
for young readers.

Yearling books feature children's
favorite authors and characters,
providing dynamic stories of adventure,
humor, history, mystery, and fantasy.

Trust Yearling paperbacks to entertain,
inspire, and promote the love of reading
in all children.

Poog

Akiko

Spuckler

Mr. Beeba

Gax

Akiko

The Training Master

Written and illustrated by

Mark Crilley

A YEARLING BOOK

To the Sensational Seto Sisters:
Elizabeth, Christina, and Katherine

Published by Yearling, an imprint of Random House Children's Books
a division of Random House, Inc., New York

Visit us on the Web! www.randomhouse.com/kids

Educators and librarians, for a variety of teaching tools, visit us at
www.randomhouse.com/teachers

ISBN-10: 0-440-41894-1
ISBN-13: 978-0-440-41894-8

Reprinted by arrangement with Delacorte Press

Printed in the United States of America

August 2006

10 9 8 7 6 5 4 3 2 1

Chapter 1

My name is Akiko. I'm a lot like most fifth-grade girls, but I'm different from all of them in at least one big way: I've got friends from another planet. A planet called Smoo.

Sounds like fun, doesn't it? It is. Mostly. The time my friends and I went to the Sprubly Islands and met Queen Pwip, for example. That was fun. Seeing all the weird animals at the Intergalactic Zoo was fun. Then there was the time I got to fly a rocket ship in a race called the Alpha Centauri 5000. That was a *lot* of fun.

But it can be pretty tough, too. In fact, sometimes having friends from Smoo means getting covered with mud, sleeping in holes, and eating some of the nastiest, slimiest, stinkiest gunk in the entire universe. I ended up doing all three not too long ago, and let me tell you, it wasn't easy. There were times when I wasn't sure I'd make it through alive.

It started a few months back, on an ordinary Saturday morning, at the Fowlerville mall.

I was shopping for blue jeans in this place called Lisa Sparx. They specialize in all kinds of neon pink and lemon yellow sequined clothes that—trust me—I wouldn't be caught dead wearing even on Halloween. For some reason, though, they sell the only kind of blue jeans I really like: blue, but not *too* blue, baggy, but not *too* baggy.

I was in the store by myself. My mom was at one of those older-lady clothing places two stores down.

It had been months since I'd hung around with my friends from the planet Smoo. Spuckler, Poog, Gax, and Mr. Beeba had dropped me off after our last adventure and blasted into space, and that was the last I'd seen of them. At first I was happy to get back to my normal daily routine at Middleton Elementary. After nearly being crushed inside the Jaws of McVluddapuck and coming within a hair of an alien-induced brainmelt, there's a lot to be said for a place where the biggest horror you face is having your favorite writing utensil chewed up by a windowsill pencil sharpener.

But as the weeks rolled by, something funny happened. I started missing the excitement. The *danger*, even. I'd had it with book reports and pop quizzes. I wanted to get back to multieyed spacemen and rusty-hulled rocket ships. Dodgeball? It has its charms, sure, but it doesn't compare to dodging Nizziks on the planet Quilk or wrangling with thramblewood on Toog. Even the cafeteria food fights didn't thrill me the way they used to. There was no getting around it: I needed an intergalactic space adventure, and I needed it soon.

But it wasn't as though I could call Spuckler on the phone or fire off an e-mail to Mr. Beeba. There was no way of getting in touch with them. I had to just sit tight and wait.

So I waited.

And waited.

Every morning on the way to school and every afternoon on the way home I kept my eyes on the sky, inspecting each passing airplane as a potential blue and red Smoovian rocket ship. Every day I checked for mysterious letters in the mail telling me they were coming to get me and instructing me to "be at your bedroom window at eight o'clock." The letters never came and neither did my friends, but every night I was at my bedroom window at eight o'clock anyway, just in case.

One day I came home from school and my mom told me there was a guy in the living room from the cable company replacing our cable box with a new one.

He could be from the cable company, I thought. *Then again, he just might be from . . .*

I ran into the living room. There he was: hunched over, his back to me, fiddling noisily with the cable box and humming an extremely tuneless tune. He had shaggy hair and, from what I could see, an unshaven chin.

"Dagnabbit!" he said, yanking furiously at a stubborn cord.

Dagnabbit? There's only one guy in the universe I know who says dagnabbit, and that's . . .

"Spuckler?" I whispered. "Spuckler! Is that you?"

"Buckler?" he said, turning to face me. He had a bushy black mustache and thick Coke-bottle glasses. Apart from the hair, the stubble on his chin, and the didn't-have-time-to-shower body odor, he was nothing like Spuckler. "Naw, little girl. Name's Floyd. Floyd Ferguson."

It was all I could do to stop from tossing my backpack to the floor in disappointment. If you're going to be a cable repairman who says dagnabbit, the least you can do is be Spuckler in disguise.

"Once *knew* a guy named Buckler," he said, turning back to wrestle with the cord. "Short bald guy with bad breath."

So here I was, several months later, shopping for

blue jeans and trying not to go crazy from the boredom of my fifth-grade life. I'd just gone into the Lisa Sparx changing room and was halfway into a pair of jeans when suddenly there was a knock on the door.

tunk tunk tunk

"Open up," said a girl's voice. "It's me."

"Me who?" I asked.

"Me *you,* that's who."

I finished putting on the jeans and opened the door. As promised, it was me. The robotic replacement me, that is: the one my friends from Smoo always brought with them to take my place while I was off in outer space having adventures.

Yes! They're back!

I poked my head out into the corridor, fully expecting to see Spuckler, Mr. Beeba, Gax, and Poog right behind her. But no: she was alone.

"Quick, get in here," I said. The robot Akiko stepped into the changing room with me and I locked the door.

"Boy, it's really great that you're here," I said.

"But you've got to be more careful. What if someone saw you?"

"Plenty of people saw me," she replied, smiling the same smile I'd seen in the mirror all my life. "Don't worry, though, Akiko. No one paid me any mind."

That's when I noticed something. The Akiko robot looked like me, all right: the *fourth-grade* me from a year ago. I'd changed a lot since then: I wasn't as round-faced anymore, and my pigtails had grown by at least three or four inches.

"This is going to be a big problem. You can't re-place me like this," I said to the robot. "You don't look like me."

"I don't?"

"Well, not *exactly* like me. See how long my pig-tails are now?"

The robot examined the length of my hair, frowned a bit, then raised her hands and grabbed her pigtails. Without so much as a wince, she pulled on them and they extended until they were the perfect length.

"Whoa," I said. "That's a very cool trick. I could really *use* hair like that. You think I could have it installed on me?"

The robot smiled. "I'll see what I can do."

It only took another minute for the Akiko robot to make the remaining adjustments—an extra inch or two in height, a slight lengthening of the face—needed to transform herself into a perfect match for me. Now she could take my place here on Earth and no one would be the wiser.

"So where are the others?" I asked her when she was done. "Don't tell me you came all the way to Earth by yourself."

"Oh, no, Akiko. They're here. They're up on the roof."

"The roof? Of the Fowlerville mall?"

"That's right." She smiled again. "They sent me rather than come down here themselves. Unlike you, they tend to attract quite a *lot* of attention."

"Yeah, tell me about it," I said. "So what's going on? Are they here to take me on another adventure?"

"You could say that," the robot replied. "Why don't you go up to the roof and find out for yourself?"

She didn't have to ask me twice. I was ready to go.

"All right, but will you be okay taking my place? My mom's—"

"At the Talbots two doors down. Don't worry. I'll find her. Just as soon as I finish buying those blue jeans you're wearing."

"Jeez, you're good at this," I said. "It's starting to get a little scary."

She gave me instructions on how to get up to the roof; then I changed back into my own jeans and let myself out of the dressing room. Within minutes I'd made my way down a dimly lit corridor in the back of the mall I'd never set foot in before, opened a door marked DO NOT OPEN! ALARM WILL SOUND! (the alarm had been deactivated by the Akiko robot), and climbed a ladder that was intended strictly for electricians and the people who clean the skylights.

I opened a door in the ceiling at the top of the ladder and pulled myself up onto the roof. It was windy and blindingly bright. A seagull squawked overhead and a gigantic air conditioner buzzed a few yards away, but otherwise it was fairly quiet. There was nothing much to see.

Until I turned and looked behind me.

There, no more than fifty feet away, stood a big, gleaming, white and yellow . . .

. . . well, it was a high-tech intergalactic train. There isn't any other way to put it. It had three separate passenger cars, a sort of locomotive-type thing at the front, and a flatbed luggage section at the back piled high with packages and suitcases. It had no wheels, which was a good thing, since there certainly wasn't any railroad track up there on the roof of the Fowlerville mall.

Through the black-tinted windows I could just make out the silhouettes of passengers. I'd seen a lot of weird aliens in my time, but some of these guys looked seriously freaky. One of them had heads where his hands should have been, and another had eyes the size of basketballs. Every car was humming quietly, momentarily cooling its jets. A strangely clean smell hung in the air, more like disinfectant than spent fuel.

PING

An electronic bell sounded and a door slid silently open at the back of the third passenger car. Out jumped Mr. Beeba and Spuckler, followed by

Gax and Poog. I was so happy to see them I was practically dancing.

" 'Kiko!" shouted Spuckler as he bounded from the train to my side in three big strides, his blue-black hair flopping around behind him and his peg leg *ch-chuck*ing every time it struck the roof. In a flash he scooped me up and gave me the biggest, stinkiest bear hug of my life, with no apparent intention of ever putting me back down. Stinky or not, it was the hug I'd been waiting ages for.

Not to be outdone, Mr. Beeba greeted me with sweeping gestures of his big yellow-gloved hands and a couple of long, fancy sentences, each packed with as many words as he could fit in.

"Truly it is an unalloyed blessing to be in your presence again, my dear. I do hope you can find it in your heart to grant us forgiveness for having failed to arrange a rendezvous with you at an earlier date."

"I'll definitely forgive you, Mr. Beeba," I replied with a wink, "as soon as I figure out what you just said."

A string of high-pitched gurgly syllables erupted beside my left ear. There was Poog hovering next to me, his purple skin glimmering in the afternoon sunlight. It was so great to see him again! I felt half ready to do some floating of my own.

"Poog says he hopes you're feeling well," said Mr. Beeba. "We've got some strenuous activity ahead of us in the days to come."

"Now that you're all here," I said, "I've never felt better."

"NOR HAVE WE, MA'AM," said Gax, rocking happily back and forth on his squeaky old wheels, his head cocked to one side on his spindly mechanical neck. "SORRY IF WE INTERRUPTED YOU IN THE MIDDLE OF SOMETHING IMPORTANT."

"Believe me, Gax. No kid has ever been in more desperate need of a nice big interruption than I am right now."

"What's the problem, 'Kiko?" asked Spuckler. "Bullies pickin' on ya? You just point 'em out to me and I'll treat 'em all to a nice big sock in th' jaw."

"No bullies, Spuckler. Just boredom. You guys have any idea how long it's been since I had any fun?"

"Well, that's all about to change, my dear," said Mr. Beeba, gesturing toward the gleaming space train behind him. "For this is the Zarga Baffa Astroshuttle, a special form of interstellar transport reserved exclusively for—"

FZIIIIT

A window slid open at the front of the locomotive and a very weird head popped out. It had about a dozen housefly eyeballs and a snout like a miniature rhinoceros.

"Ig! Ig!" it said from a mouth I couldn't see. *"Ig-f'-griddle-gick!"*

"Oh, dear," said Mr. Beeba, taking me by the arm. "It seems we're putting the conductor behind schedule. We'd better get on board before he makes good on his threat to leave us behind."

We all piled into the third passenger car as quickly as we could. I got one last glimpse of the mall's roof before the door slid shut and the Zarga Baffa Astroshuttle rose noiselessly into the air.

Chapter 2

There wasn't space to breathe, let alone sit down. Mr. Beeba instructed me to grab hold of a metallic strap hanging from the ceiling, and I did so just in time to steady myself as the vessel began to pick up speed. On the other side of the windows Fowlerville fell away, and soon we were up above the clouds, gaining mile upon mile of altitude with each passing second.

"So what's the mission this time?" I asked Mr. Beeba.

"It's not a mission," Mr. Beeba replied. "It's something much better than that. King Froptoppit has this day bestowed upon us an honor unlike any other. We are to join the others in this vessel as the newest class of students enrolled in the Intergalactic Space Patrollers Training Camp on Zarga Baffa."

"A training camp?" I said. "Cool. What kind of stuff are they going to teach us there?"

"THE ZARGA BAFFA TRAINING METHOD IS SHROUDED IN MYSTERY," said Gax. "GRADUATES ARE INSTRUCTED NOT TO DESCRIBE IT IN DETAIL. BUT THEY SAY SOME EXERCISES INVOLVE VERY REAL LIFE-OR-DEATH SITUATIONS: LASER BATTLES AGAINST HORRIBLE MONSTERS, PARACHUTING FROM SPEEDING ROCKET SHIPS . . ."

"I dunno about the rest of ya," said Spuckler, "but I'm mainly in this for the Drugollian kickboxing lessons. I hear they teach ya moves that'll bring a whole gang of skazzle-backed bluck beasts to their knees."

"Man, this sounds like a pretty wild place," I said. "So what exactly *are* space patrollers, anyway? What do they do?"

"THEY ARE THE FIRST LINE OF DEFENSE AGAINST

THE VILLAINS OF THE UNIVERSE," said Gax. "EVERY PLANET IN THE UNIVERSE NEEDS ITS OWN CREW OF SPACE PATROLLERS TO DEFEND ITSELF AGAINST INTERSTELLAR THIEVES AND BANDITS. SADLY, THE PLANET SMOO HAS NEVER HAD SUCH A CREW."

"Dreadful bad luck," said Mr. Beeba. "King Froptoppit has sent many a band of would-be space patrollers to Zarga Baffa, only to have all of them rejected prior to graduation. The last group he sent did so poorly the training masters of Zarga Baffa said they could accept no further trainees from Smoo. King Froptoppit prevailed upon them for one last chance. We," he added with a raised finger, "are that last chance."

"Wow," I said. "There's a lot riding on this."

"I'll say there is," said Mr. Beeba. "If we fail to become certified space patrollers, King Froptoppit's disappointment will be beyond words. Indeed, the entire population of Smoo is counting on us."

I glanced at Poog. He was smiling proudly, confident in our chances of success. There was a trace of nervousness in his eyes, though, as if he knew the road ahead would be long and hard.

"Well, we can't let King Froptoppit down," I said, clapping my hands together. "I mean, come on, we've been through some pretty bad scrapes, the five of us. We're as ready to be space patrollers as anyone else in this ship."

I glanced around at our fellow passengers. Immediately to my left was a yellow-green guy with a tiny head and three beady eyes. He had arms that hung all the way down to the floor, looped around a few times, then crisscrossed up to his face, where they turned the pages of a small book: judging from the illustration on the cover, it was a how-to guide for a long-armed brand of kung fu. He didn't make a sound, but he pried his eyes away from his book long enough to shoot me a glance that said "Who you lookin' at?"

I turned my attention to a passenger standing just behind me. She—well, she *looked* like a she, anyway—was about two feet tall, with spiky green hair and a tiny pink-lipsticked mouth. She was dressed in a red leather suit with a see-through space helmet over her head, and was scrawling notes on a pad of paper as she watched a series of grainy images flash by on a nearby video monitor.

"So these are the other trainees, right?" I said to Mr. Beeba. "Looks like they're just as determined to graduate as we are."

"But of course," said Mr. Beeba. "Official space patroller status is a distinction coveted by people all across the universe, from royals on the moons of Glissflik to peasants on the rings of Smaturn."

"Don't you mean the rings of *Sat*urn?" I said.

Mr. Beeba's face twitched a bit, then settled into a frown. "I meant what I said, Akiko. Smaturn is a densely populated planet in the Zoodi galaxy, whereas the planet of which you are speaking is *entirely* uninhabited." He snorted loudly. "But maybe you know something I don't," he added, signaling with his eyes that I definitely didn't.

I gazed out the windows as we zoomed across the sea of stars, then examined the faces of our fellow passengers, one at a time. Some looked excited, others looked scared, but one thing's for sure: no one looked bored.

Something Mr. Beeba had said echoed in my

head. "The entire population of Smoo is counting on us." I imagined ordinary Smoovian families in their homes, anxiously waiting for word from Zarga Baffa. I pictured King Froptoppit pacing the floors of his palace, wondering if we would succeed or fail.

We can't mess this up, I thought. *We've got to graduate from this training camp. No matter what it takes.*

Chapter 3

A few hours later we arrived on the planet Zarga Baffa. It was big and not quite round: like a pyramid with its edges rubbed smooth. As we approached, the passengers tapped their claws and tentacles on the windows and chattered among themselves. One fish-eyed alien worked herself up into such a frenzy she nearly fainted. I felt like the only one on board who hadn't been dreaming of this moment for years.

Still, I was excited. I couldn't wait for our first lesson to begin.

The Zarga Baffa Astroshuttle rocketed into the planet's upper atmosphere and glided down through the clouds until we were treated to a dazzling view of rolling pink hills, strange purple trees, and towering yellow mountains as smooth and pointy as sharks' teeth. Zarga Baffa was beautiful and weird, like a coral-covered landscape at the bottom of the ocean.

After a few more minutes we entered a lush valley where a vast complex of glass buildings came into view. It was at least fifty miles from one side to the other, with a single dome in the center big enough to cover an entire city. The babbling of the passengers died away as the train coasted into a station just inside one of several smaller domes. We came to a stop near a purple-carpeted platform lined with marble statues of multiheaded heroes, potted plants, and silver urns overflowing with brightly colored flowers.

PING

The doors slid open and we all bustled out of the astroshuttle. Between the yellow-green guy's arms flopping all over the place and the little red-suited lady with the space helmet dashing to get past me, it's a miracle I didn't fall and smack my head on the ground.

A man employed by the training camp—tall, gray-skinned, and dressed entirely in white— instructed the passengers to form a line along one side of the platform. Mr. Beeba followed his every word, seeing to it that Spuckler, Gax, Poog, and I got to our proper places.

"You might want to take a moment to think of a greeting for our training master," Mr. Beeba said to me. "I would suggest something along the lines of 'Thank you, O wise and learned one, for wasting your valuable energies on so feeble a wretch as I.' "

"You've got to be kidding," I said.

"Come to think of it, forget I said 'something along the lines of.' You'll be better off saying that word for word."

"Uh-huh. So what's a training master? Some kind of teacher?"

"MORE THAN THAT, MA'AM," said Gax. "HE OR SHE WILL HAVE ABSOLUTE CONTROL OVER OUR LIVES FOR THE NEXT THREE WEEKS. THE CENTRAL PILLAR OF THE ZARGA BAFFA METHOD IS ONE'S UNQUESTION-ING FAITH IN THE TRAINING MASTER."

I wasn't so sure what to think of this. Being

under someone's absolute control didn't sound like a whole lot of fun.

DWUNNNNNnnnnnnnnnnnnnnnng

There was a loud gonging sound and the trainees silenced themselves.

"Stand up straight, Akiko," whispered Mr. Beeba. "Our training masters are coming out to greet us."

As the last echo of the gong faded away, it was replaced by strains of soft, stately music, high-pitched and mysterious, like a slow march performed on muted, alien bagpipes. All eyes turned to a pair of tall brass doors at the far end of the platform, flanked by two guards dressed in spotless white and yellow uniforms.

I had been pretty excited to begin with, but now my heart was really thumping. What kind of training master would we get?

The music continued for another minute or two while we waited and waited, the anticipation building. Finally the first in the procession of training masters emerged from the shadows of the doorway.

There were twenty in all. They each wore simple black clothing with golden bands around the waist and wrists. They came in all shapes and sizes, some human, some nearly human, others more like lizards waddling on their hind legs, and at least one that glided over the ground like an elegant snail. Some of them had long beards, and a few walked with canes. They all carried themselves with great dignity, projecting wisdom and grace with every step they took.

A really tall one walked straight toward us. He had big, fierce eyes and a thin-lipped mouth that looked more comfortable with frowns than smiles. I let out a big sigh of relief when he pivoted on one heel and crossed to a different group of trainees.

When all the training masters had found their places, a wrinkled old man with a long blue mustache stepped to a podium at the side of the platform and spoke. "I am Odo Mumzibar," he said, "the current headmaster of the Zarga Baffa Training Camp. It is my privilege to welcome you here today. No matter where you have come from, no matter what innate skills you may or may not possess, I promise you that three weeks hence you will emerge from this training camp stronger and more capable in every respect.

"It won't come easily, though," said Odo Mumzibar, his bushy blue eyebrows drawn into an expression of great seriousness. "You will be tested here at Zarga Baffa, pushed to your limits, made to do things you have never done before. If ever you find yourself troubled by any aspect of your training, please feel free to come directly to me."

He raised a finger, leaned forward, and studied the faces of the trainees. "I have only one piece of advice for all of you," he said, "and it is simply this: never give up." He paused for a very long time, and I felt sure that he would follow these words with an explanation, or a story, or, I don't know, *something*. But instead, he simply leaned closer to the microphone and repeated himself: "Never give up."

He stood straight, cleared his throat, and said, "Students, meet your training masters." Odo

Mumzibar then stepped down from the podium and disappeared through the double doors.

One by one the training masters bowed to their new pupils and led them away. Mr. Beeba, Spuckler, Poog, Gax, and I were the only students still on the platform. A light breeze whistled past, and a dead leaf dropped from one of the potted plants. As we watched the last of the training masters disappear from view, it dawned on us that we weren't getting one.

The guards shot each other uncomfortable glances as the music came to a stop and the astro-shuttle quietly floated off, turned a corner, and disappeared. I had the peculiar feeling of being the last person picked when teams were divvied up in gym class. Only worse.

Then the *pat-pat-pat* of hasty footsteps came echoing from the doorway and out came one last training master, the youngest of them all, out of breath and wiping sweat from his forehead.

"Sorry I'm late," he said, clearing his throat and

running a hand through his long red-brown hair. "My last class ran a little over schedule."

He was small but stocky, with dark, authoritative eyebrows and slightly crooked teeth. His eyes were wide set, narrow, and tinged a bright shade of violet. They were pinched into an apologetic squint at the moment, but there was no masking the confidence behind them. "I may be young," they seemed to say, "but that doesn't mean I'm inexperienced."

"I'm Chibb Fallaby, your training master for the next three weeks."

"Pleased t' meetcha, Chibb," said Spuckler, thrusting out his arm for a vigorous handshake. "Spuckler Boach is the name, but you can call me Spuck."

"Hello, Spuck," said Chibb. "Good to have you on board."

Mr. Beeba lurched forward and bowed extravagantly. "Thank you, O wise and learned one," he said so stiffly it sounded as if he were preparing to sing a hymn, "for wasting your—"

"Now, now," said Chibb. "Don't worry about formalities with me. I like my students to think of me as a friend."

Mr. Beeba stuttered a bit and answered, "I—I wholeheartedly approve. Formalities are . . . ever so tiresome." He coughed and added: "I am Mr. Beeba, at your service."

"A pleasure to make your acquaintance, Mr. Beeba."

"I HOPE YOU DON'T OBJECT TO HAVING A ROBOT AMONG YOUR STUDENTS," said Gax. "ESPECIALLY AN OLDER MODEL LIKE MYSELF."

"Certainly not," said Chibb, patting Gax on the

helmet. "I've trained robots many times before. They make some of the best students, actually, the older models in particular. They're far less likely to act like know-it-alls and are astonishingly good at facts and figures." Gax was so happy he was nearly bouncing on his shock absorbers.

Poog floated forward and spoke in his warbly, high-pitched language. Chibb bowed and replied, "It's certainly an honor to have a Toogolian here on Zarga Baffa. We get so few of them. But surely *you* should be the training master, Poog, and I the student."

No way, I thought. *He understands Toogolian.*

Poog smiled and added a gurgly word or two.

"Very well, then," answered Chibb. "I shall do my best." He then turned his attention to me.

"Now, you must be Akiko," he said. "King Frop-toppit spoke very highly of you when he arranged for your enrollment. 'The brightest star in the Milky Way,' he called you."

I felt my face grow warm. "I'm just . . . a kid," I

replied, wishing I could think of something more interesting to say.

"Ah, but you're more than that," he said with a flash of his crooked teeth. "You are the very first Earthian ever to attend this training camp. I'm sure you will be a credit to your planet."

"Uh, thanks."

His purple eyes were warm and friendly as he took my hand in his. It seemed to me at that moment that we had lucked into the best training master in all of Zarga Baffa.

Chapter 4

Chibb led us through the shadowy doorway and into a cavernous space beyond, where moving sidewalks and whooshing hovercraft carried students from one part of the training camp to another. He launched into a guided tour as he walked, singing the praises of the Zarga Baffa method and listing the accomplishments of the camp's famous former students.

"... and then of course there's Z'makk Vafftron, from the planet Nulu. They say he was scared stiff of space travel when he first came here. Couldn't go to the nearest moon without gritting his teeth and keeping his eyes shut. Now he commands a whole fleet of voltex cruisers for the Ambulan guard."

A high-tech door rose noiselessly into the ceiling and we passed into a section where students were soaking in hot, steamy baths and being massaged by multiarmed aliens in white and yellow uniforms. There was a gigantic swimming pool—at least ten times larger than Olympic size—and several dozen Jacuzzi-type tubs, all bubbling and gurgling with milky, warm water. Everyone in the room looked thoroughly relaxed, in the very best of health.

Awesome, I thought. *I wonder if we can extend the three weeks.*

"Maintaining the body is at the very core of our guiding principles," said Chibb. "So is stimulating the mind."

Another door slid silently into the wall and we entered a great hall that looked like a beautiful library in a luxurious old castle. Students read and sipped from teacups while reclining in the glow of a gigantic stone hearth in the center of the room, where a bright turquoise fire blazed. Self-propelled book carts glided around the room, allowing students to browse without rising from their comfy leather chairs. Mr. Beeba looked as if he'd died and gone to heaven.

"Of course, healthy minds and bodies require good food," said Chibb as he led us into the spacious, airy Zarga Baffa cafeteria, "and we'll see to it that you get *plenty* of it during your stay here."

I gazed around at students dining on an endless variety of exotic dishes: great bubbling bowls of silvery soup; plates piled high with blue and orange noodles, flowery multicolored vegetables, and golden-crusted fish so long from head to tail they snaked from platter to platter and from one table to another. And the aromas! Sweet, spicy, smoked, and sautéed in butter—every smell I'd ever hungered for and plenty I'd never encountered in my life. It was all I could do to stop myself from abandoning the group to sneak a bite.

After we left the cafeteria Chibb led us around a corner and down a flight of stairs. There was less light, and the air felt colder, damper.

"You're going to love it here, I'm sure of it," said Chibb. He came to a door that didn't slide sideways or rise into the ceiling but simply screeched open on a pair of rusty hinges. "All trainees do, once they've survived Humbling Week."

"H-Humbling Week?" Mr. Beeba said. We were now in a dark, musty corridor with weakly flickering lightbulbs dangling from the ceiling. I wanted to walk more slowly because it was hard to see the floor, and what I *could* see of it seemed to be a happy home for roaches, worms, and worse. But Chibb was walking faster than before, and seemed to increase his speed with every step.

"But of course. Those places I just showed you are for the advanced trainees only. You've got to get through Humbling Week before you'll have access to any of that. I'm sure you read all about it in the brochure."

"B-brochure?" Mr. Beeba said.

Chibb turned and cocked his head with a look of mild surprise. "Don't tell me you didn't get a brochure." He then stepped forward and heaved his weight against another door, this one even rustier than the first. "I'll have to talk to the folks in admissions about that."

We stumbled through the doorway and found ourselves outdoors. The air was bitterly cold. The sun had sunk so low in the sky the only trace of its glow left was on the very top branches of grizzled, leafless trees towering above us. Chibb picked up the pace and led us down a rough gravelly sidewalk that grew more and more potholed and crumbly with every step. He was soon walking so quickly we had to jog just to keep up with him.

"Say, Chibb," said Spuckler. "Where in the heck're ya takin' us?"

"Why, to your holes, of course."

"H-holes?" said Mr. Beeba.

"You'll be sleeping in holes tonight," said Chibb. "*And* tomorrow night. And the next. And the four nights after that. We call it the Seven Nights of Mud and Misery. They go hand in hand with the Seven Days of Strain and Struggle. Together they comprise Humbling Week." He paused to leap over an enormous fallen tree trunk in the middle of the path. "It's all about stripping away the layers of pride and overconfidence that plague inexperienced trainees."

Poog and Gax exchanged puzzled glances. They

were probably thinking the same thing I was: that the whole thing must be some sort of big mistake.

"But we're not inexperienced," I said. "We've rescued people before, and taken care of bad guys too."

Chibb turned to me without breaking his stride, chuckled, and shook his head. To my astonishment he ignored my comment altogether. "By the end of the week you'll all have been ground down into powdery little wisps of your former selves. It's unpleasant, to be sure. Almost unbearable, actually. But it's a crucial part of our operation." He came to a stop and gestured to the path ahead of us, which rose almost vertically to the top of a fifty-foot hill. "This is as far as I can take you. So long. Grunn Grung will bring your evening meal."

He turned and strutted back down the path without waving goodbye.

"Gr-Grunn Grung?" Mr. Beeba said.

"You'll love him," said Chibb without turning around. "*Everyone* loves Grunn Grung." It was hard to tell if he was joking.

Chapter 5

"I assure you . . . *ngh* . . . King Froptoppit told me nothing . . . *oooph* . . . about Humbling Week," said Mr. Beeba as we began to negotiate the nightmarish path to the top of the hill. It was a mix of thick mud and sharp-edged stones, as if it had been calculated to make you slide two steps backward for every step forward, and to slice your elbows up in the process.

"Aw, quit yer moanin'," said Spuckler, who—though he had Gax tucked under one arm—was farther up the hill than the rest of us. "I think ol' Chibb's got it right. A kick in th' pants is just what we need. Roughin' it for a spell never hurt nobody."

Mr. Beeba groaned, as if to prove that it was already hurting him quite a lot.

"IT WON'T BE LONG NOW," said Gax, craning his spindly neck to monitor our progress. "WE'RE ONLY TWENTY-SEVEN AND ONE-THIRD METERS FROM THE TOP."

Poog, who could have floated straight to the top of the hill if he'd wanted to, chose instead to stay at my side, humming quietly to himself. I turned and gave him a smile. Based on what Chibb had said about Humbling Week, I knew I'd need all the moral support Poog had to offer.

It took us at least half an hour to get to the top of the hill. When we got there—bruised, bleeding, and sopping wet with icy-cold mud—an infuriating discovery awaited us: the other side of the hill was nothing more than wooden scaffolding with a rickety stairway leading straight back down to the ground. The "hill" was an artificial obstacle. It was carefully designed to guarantee that a grueling half hour of pain and suffering always stood between us and a good night's sleep.

"Well, I'll be ding-dong-daggled," said Spuckler. He was inspecting a pipe that spat an endless stream of cold water down the path, ensuring that it stayed muddy at all times. "These fellers mean business."

"I don't care *what* they mean," said Mr. Beeba, already making his way down the stairway. "*I* mean to have a nice hot shower and get a good night's rest."

I had no idea what awaited us at the end of the path, but I was pretty sure it wouldn't be hot showers. I wiped as much of the mud from my face as I could and dragged my aching body down the stairs, one step at a time.

The path continued for about a quarter mile before abruptly plunging into a marshy dead end. On the other side of a swamp (one that I suspected had been artificially created by the same people who had built the hill) stood a rough stone wall carved out of the side of a cliff. In the wall were several dozen holes of varying shapes and sizes.

We trudged the last mushy yards through the swamp and crawled up onto the narrow patch of dry land at the base of the wall. From here we could see that most of the holes were occupied by other beginners like ourselves, some of whom I recognized from the astroshuttle. The yellow-green guy was already there, fast asleep in a hole near the ground. The little woman with the red leather suit was also there, seated on the edge of a hole farther up, furiously trying to get dried mud off her boots. From every hole came moans of pain and exhaustion.

"You know what?" I said. "The Fowlerville mall is starting to sound pretty nice right about now."

"Hey, c'mon, 'Kiko," said Spuckler. "Buck up. We gotta show these Zarga Baffa guys we ain't a bunch of wimps." He led the way to a cluster of five empty holes reserved for us. "Now, which hole d'ya want? I call this big'un over here."

The "big" one was no more than three feet in diameter. As it turned out, Spuckler had to give up that hole for Gax, who wouldn't fit into any of the others. I chose a midsized hole—about two feet across at its widest—and took a peek inside. By this point the sky was so dark I could barely see a thing, but there wasn't much to see anyway. It was a hole and nothing more, lined on all sides with cold, damp stones, with no pillow or bedding of any kind. I swallowed hard and started to crawl inside.

BROOOOOoooo

A bloodcurdling howl echoed down to us from the top of the wall. I was torn between climbing back out of my hole to get a better look and crawling farther in to hide. I compromised by crawling all the way in and then poking just my head out. What I saw made me wish the holes had doors that could be slammed shut and locked.

There, making its way down the wall, was an enormous brown slug creature covered with patches of bloodred fur. It was about the size of a buffalo, and able to move vertically across the wall by way of its sticky underside. It had eight long, spindly arms with clawed hands at the tips, four of which clutched small wooden buckets.

"Twenty gilpots says that's Grunn Grung," said Spuckler. No one took him up on the bet. We all knew it was Grunn Grung, just as surely as we knew that whatever was sloshing around in those buckets would turn out to be our dinner.

BROOOOOoooo

Grunn Grung slithered from place to place, tossing the buckets into our holes so recklessly you'd have thought he intended to spill as much of the contents as he could. When he reached my hole and slapped the bucket inside, he slid his head in after it and stared at me. His eyes were black and beady, held in place by wrinkled folds of slimy flesh. His mouth was toothless, round, and dripping with saliva.

"Eeeeaaaaat noowww," he whispered, his voice hoarse and choked with spittle. "Beeefooore it getsss cooooold."

This, I soon realized, was Grunn Grung's attempt at a little joke: the porridge-thick stew of bluish gray sludge was ice-cold and—from what I could tell—had never been heated to begin with.

"Taaaaa taaaaa," he said before his head receded from view. I caught one last glimpse of him before he vanished over the top of the wall; then I decided to check on the others.

"Mr. Beeba! Are you all right?"

"If that hideous creature is gone for good," came

his answer from a hole to my left, "then yes, my condition is satisfactory for the moment."

"Gax? Poog?"

Gax's head emerged from his hole and rotated until it faced me. "I AM QUITE ALL RIGHT, MA'AM. THESE DAMP CONDITIONS HAVE WROUGHT A BIT OF HAVOC WITH MY CARBURETOR, BUT APART FROM THAT I REALLY HAVE NOTHING TO COMPLAIN ABOUT."

Poog floated out of his hole and gurgled a brief warbly reply. His face was spattered with mud, but he seemed to be in good spirits.

"Spuckler?"

"Say, this stuff ain't so bad," said Spuckler, poking his head out from where he lay two holes beneath me, his chin dribbled with stew. "I've had worse than this. *Plenty* worse."

I raised the mildewed old bucket to my nose and took a whiff. The contents smelled like an old dog that had been rolling in a pile of rotting vegetables. Hungry as I was, there was no way I'd be eating this stuff.

I poked my head out of the hole, then snuck down to Spuckler, bucket in hand.

"Spuckler," I whispered into his little cave. "You want this?"

Spuckler looked shocked. "Now, listen, 'Kiko. Like it or not, you gotta eat. We got a long, hard day ahead of us tomorrow. You'll never make it through on an empty stomach."

"I'm sorry, Spuckler. I can't put this stuff in my mouth. It'll make me sick."

Spuckler regarded me for a moment longer. He must have seen that I wasn't going to change my mind.

"All right. Have it your way. But don't come whining to me when you're half starved tomorrow afternoon."

"Good night, Spuckler."

"G'night, 'Kiko."

Just then a voice echoed down from above: "Hey, you!"

I turned to see the green long-armed guy glaring down at me from his hole, his three eyes glowing angrily. Behind him were the heads of four tough-looking aliens, the other members of his trainee crew. "Back to bed! You're going to get us all in trouble!"

"Sorry," I said. "I didn't know there was a rule against—"

"Hey, listen," he said before I could finish, "*I didn't know* doesn't cut it around here. You just watch yourself, kiddo."

"All right, all right," I said, scaling the mossy wall as quickly as I could. "My name is not 'kiddo,' by the way. It's Akiko."

"Friends call me Dregger. That means *you* call me sir."

"Nice to meet you," I said before crawling back into my hole. I was trying to be polite, but I'm sure he knew that meeting him was anything but nice.

Dregger said nothing in return. But then, a moment later, he whispered to one of his friends, loudly enough for me to hear: "Earthians: they're all scrawny and snot-brained."

I wanted to say something mean in return but

decided against it. *Better just ignore him. I don't want to make any enemies my first night.*

Lying on my side, I rolled myself up to conserve as much body heat as possible. My jeans and T-shirt were soaked with mud, and every minute or two a frigid gust of wind blew straight in on top of me. I'd have given anything for a blanket right then, or even just a bath towel.

All this mud and misery is for a good reason, I told myself. *King Froptoppit needs us to graduate and become Smoo's first space patrollers. If I can just stay focused on that I'll be okay.*

I closed my eyes and thought of Chibb. He'd seemed like such a nice guy when we'd first met him. Now I wasn't so sure.

I shuddered when it occurred to me that we hadn't even made it through a full day yet. Seven days. Seven long days.

If I can make it through this, I can make it through anything, I thought.

I rolled over and tried to get to sleep.

Chapter 6

After what felt like just a few hours of sleep, a piercing squeal blasted me awake. I opened my eyes to find it was still pitch black outside, and very, very cold. Sticking my head out of the hole, I saw Grunn Grung at the base of the wall, holding a torch and blowing into a long, curved horn.

"He's got to be kidding," I said. "It's the middle of the night."

I rubbed my eyes and stared in amazement at the other students climbing eagerly out of their holes for the first day of training. They were all wide awake, as if they had no need for sleep.

"C'mon, 'Kiko!" shouted Spuckler. "Look alive!"

By the time I'd climbed down from my hole, all the others had lined up behind Grunn Grung and begun marching through the swamp to get back to the training center. I took my place at the end of the line and braced myself for the icy-cold waters of the swamp. Since my clothes had only just begun to dry, it was heartbreaking to get them wet again.

"ONE NIGHT DOWN," said Gax, trying to sound encouraging, "ONLY SIX TO GO."

Grunn Grung led us all through a tunnel in the artificial hill (they evidently reserved making us climb it for the end of the day, when it would exhaust us the most) and bid us farewell on the other side.

"Tooooniiiight," he said to me as I marched away, stretching his toothless mouth into an ugly smile, "yoooou wiiiill eeeeat."

Don't bet on it, I thought. I was already hungry from the missed meal, though; there was no denying it.

After marching back down the long, crumbly path, we all eventually wound up in a place called the Gathering Plaza, a wide circle of concrete just outside the training masters' quarters. I rubbed my arms and hoped that the sun—only now making its way over the horizon—would warm me up in a hurry. Everyone stood at attention as the training masters emerged from their front door and rejoined their assigned students. Chibb was the last to arrive.

"Breakfast," he said to us without smiling as he opened a sack and handed each of us a black lump that had the look and feel of a piece of coal.

Spuckler tore into it with gusto, while Mr. Beeba and I nibbled more cautiously. It took me three bites to determine that it was indeed food, a further three to discern that it had flavor (it wasn't the least bit salty or sweet, but possessed a faint trace of bitterness), and a final three to decide that it was some sort of bland, rock-hard bread.

"All right," said Chibb before any of us had finished. "Enough standing around. Off to our first lessons."

Without another word he led us back into the Zarga Baffa complex and through about a dozen different corridors. Finally we arrived at a vast space with a sloping glass ceiling like a greenhouse. The floor was covered with rolling hills of grass and flowers, everything glowing orange with the first rays of morning sunlight. After all the mud and misery it felt great to be in such a beautiful place. The fresh, clean air was enough to make me feel a little better about Zarga Baffa.

"Before we begin," said Chibb, "I just want to make sure you all know about crying blue."

"Crying blue?" said Mr. Beeba. "That's the Zarga Baffian term for quitting, isn't it?"

"Indeed," said Chibb. "It's a good deal more than simply quitting, though. When a trainee cries blue, he or she admits complete and utter defeat. If you feel that you cannot endure even a single second more of

Humbling Week, the solution to your troubles is as simple as can be: just shout out the word *blue* as loudly as you can, and your training will instantly come to an end. You will be sent back to your home planet while the rest of your crew carries on without you."

"Blue?" I asked. "Why blue?"

"It goes back to Hubbly Golgiddy, the first Zarga Baffa student to abandon his training. Hubbly was making his way through one of our obstacle courses when he fell headfirst into a vat of blue slime. For whatever reason, that was the breaking point for him, and he gave up his training then and there. The sight of Hubbly Golgiddy weeping and covered in blue slime became the very image of a quitter in the minds of trainees and training masters alike. And so it is that when trainees quit, we say they have cried blue."

He gave us all a look of great seriousness.

"But remember this: crying blue is an indelible mark of shame, a stain on your character that will haunt you for the rest of your life. You will be known until your dying day as feeble and weak, a person of little consequence. Such is the fate of one who cries blue on Zarga Baffa."

I swallowed hard and folded my arms, making sure Chibb saw the toughest-looking Akiko possible.

There's no way I'm going to cry blue, I thought. *I don't care how bad it gets.*

Chapter 7

Chibb directed our attention to the field before us. "We'll start with something simple: a test of motor skills called the Yoodoo Egg Rescue."

Spuckler's eyes lit up. "Ya mean ya got a yoodoo bird here?"

"We do indeed, Spuck."

"Mighty tasty bird."

"We *won't* be eating it, I assure you." Chibb pointed to a blue and yellow speck at the far end of the dome. "Over there is the mother yoodoo bird, waiting in her nest."

I shielded my eyes from the morning sun and tried my best to make out the shapes of a nest and bird. The distance forced me to use my imagination.

Chibb then pointed to three blue objects in three different parts of the pasture. "The eggs are there . . . there . . . and there."

One of them was close enough to see quite clearly. It was about the size of a basketball. Its surface was sky blue with yellow spots, and very glossy.

"And that's about it, really," said Chibb, clapping his hands together. "Pick up the eggs, carry them across the field, and put them in the nest. You've got to do it all in one trip."

"That doesn't look so hard," I said.

Chibb snapped his head to one side and stared at me with a look of surprise and mild annoyance.

"Oh, it doesn't, does it?" It was as if I'd insulted a member of his family. "Well, perhaps you'd like to go first, then."

I looked at the others. Spuckler was grinning a go-for-it grin. Mr. Beeba and Gax shivered as if they thought I was making a big, big mistake. Poog smiled and nodded approvingly. He had a slightly worried look in his eyes, though.

"Sure," I said, doing my best to sound confident. "Someone's got to go first. Why not me?"

"Be my guest," said Chibb, pulling a silver stopwatch from his pocket. "You've got three minutes." His smile was definitely hiding something. "Starting . . ." He lifted the stopwatch to his eyes. "Now!"

I tore off across the field as quickly as I could. First I had to go up and over a gentle hill. The ground was a bit soft, making it hard to run at top speed, but otherwise I could see nothing to stop me from getting those eggs to the nest in well under three minutes. Two minutes, tops.

I arrived at the first egg, lifted it, and tucked it under my right arm. It was about as heavy as a gallon of milk. Not enough to slow me down, not by a long shot. I was halfway to the second egg when . . .

Sssssssssssshhhhhhhh

POOOOAM

. . . something struck the ground somewhere behind me. I spun to see an enormous red boulder half submerged in the field just beyond the hill, smoke billowing up from it in big black clouds. It was a meteor, freshly fallen from the sky.

Through the smoke I could just make out the face of Chibb Fallaby, who was smiling and chuckling to himself. He consulted his stopwatch and shouted: "Two minutes, forty-five seconds left! Better get a move on!"

Sssssssssssssssssshhhhhhhh

POOOOOOOAM

A second meteor struck the ground, this time off to my left, but considerably closer than the first. I followed the trail of smoke up to a chute at the center of the glass ceiling. A third meteor had already emerged and was on its way down. This time it looked as though it was heading straight toward me.

I ran as fast as I could without dropping the egg, realizing too late that I was actually heading back toward Chibb and the others.

Sssssssssssssssssssshhhhhhhh

POOOOOOOOOAM

It missed me by a good ten yards. But if I hadn't moved, it could easily have landed right on top of me.

"Only two and a half minutes left!" Chibb shouted. "You're pushing it!"

"What—" I began, then switched to the only question that mattered to me at the moment: "Are they *real?*"

Chibb grinned and kept his eyes on the stop-watch. He was fiddling with it for some reason, as if it needed winding or something. "They're real enough."

Real enough? What is that supposed to mean?

"I'd keep moving if I were you," said Chibb, point-ing up at the chute. "It's almost finished reloading!"

"C'mon, 'Kiko!" hollered Spuckler. "Show him whatcher made of!"

I turned, located the second egg, then sprinted toward it, dividing my attention between the ground ahead and the sky above. Sure enough, more meteors were already on their way, this time two of them at once.

Sssssssssssssssssssshhhhhhhh

The first was coming straight down into the path in front of me. I changed direction just in time.

POOOOOOOOOAM

Sssssssssssssssssssssshhhhhhhh

The second had looked like it was heading toward the same spot as the first, but then—was it my imagination?—it seemed to change direction in midair. Now it was rocketing straight to where I stood! Clutching the egg as hard as I could, I leaped to one side and somersaulted out of the way.

POOOOOOOOOOOOAM

This is insane. They're following me!

There was a brief break in the meteor shower. It was almost as if the meteors were waiting for me to get up on my feet again.

"Two minutes!" shouted Chibb.

I've got to at least get the second egg. If I don't I'll be a complete reject.

I took off again, this time cutting and weaving unpredictably through the field, all the while moving steadily closer to the second egg.

Ssssssshhhhhh POOOOAM

Sssssssssshhhhhhh POOOOOAM

The meteors began raining down again, fast and furious. They were crashing into the field all around me. I dashed, dodged, leaped, and lurched: whatever it took to get to that egg without turning into meteor meat in the process.

ShhPOAMshhhPOOAMshhhhPOOOAM

Finally—miraculously—I made it to the second egg and scooped it into my left arm. That's when I realized . . .

. . . I had absolutely no idea how I was going to carry the third egg.

"One and a half minutes!" I heard Chibb call from far away.

This is impossible. Impossible!

I located the third egg. It wasn't that far off, but under the circumstances it might as well have been light-years away. How was I supposed to pick the thing up? Sprout a third arm?

"Move, child!" came Chibb's voice from far away behind me.

Did he just call me "child"?

"Mooovc!"

ShhhhPOAMshhhPOAMshhhhhhhPOAM

Meteors pounded the field on all sides as I sprinted back and forth, cutting a wild, jagged path through the tall grass. Holding both eggs meant that I no longer had the full movement of my arms, which made it really hard to maintain my balance. The added weight was slowing me down too. Suddenly, just four feet to my right . . .

ShhhhhhhhhBOOOOOOOOOOOOOOOOM!

. . . a meteor the size of a minivan thundered into the grass. The ground rocked as it exploded like a bomb within inches of me. The air was thick with plumes of black smoke and the stench of burning grass, and my skin burned as if it were being roasted over a bonfire. I came to a complete stop and just stared at the thing, dumbstruck. It had almost flattened me: if I'd been any farther to the left, I'd have been so completely obliterated it would have been as if I'd never even existed. That was when my strength—and my will to go on—gave out altogether: I totally lost what little nerve I had left.

Crouching down and whimpering like a two-year-old, I shut my eyes and prepared to be vaporized by the next meteor out of the chute. Seconds passed—who knew how many—but . . .

. . . the next meteor never arrived.

I opened my eyes.

All was silent. There, no more than three yards in front of me, was the third egg.

"Hey!" came Chibb's shout. "Are you going to get up off the ground and go *get* that thing, or am I going to have to do it for you?"

I rose cautiously and began taking the final steps to the third egg.

"C'mon! Go! Go! Go!" Chibb sounded furious. "You've got thirty seconds!"

When I got to the spot where the third egg lay, I did the only thing I could do: I lowered myself and tried picking it up with my knees. To my amazement I found that I was able to lift it with ease, and could even straighten up to a large degree without dropping it.

Moving forward, however, was a different story.

I wobbled precariously one step at a time, inching my way across the final thirty-odd yards between the nest and me. I tried moving more quickly, but the third egg started slipping and I had to slow down again.

"Twenty seconds!" shouted Chibb. *"Move!"*

Sweat poured down my face and back. My

heart was pounding and my legs were starting to cramp up.

I raised my head and got my first good look at the mother yoodoo bird: she was blue and yellow, with a big floppy crest on her head like a rooster. She watched me for a moment, yawned, and turned her attention to rearranging sticks in her nest.

"Ten seconds!"

The meteors had stopped entirely, as if they knew I had more than enough problems at the moment and had decided to cut me some slack.

I wobbled forward with all the energy I had left. There were no more than twenty yards to go, but with so little time I knew I'd never make it.

"Five!"

I stopped and slowly sank to the ground, letting go of all three eggs and watching them roll into the grass around me.

"Three . . . two . . . one . . ."

BLAAAAYUUUUUUUNG

A huge, booming noise echoed across the field, low and sad, like a chorus of foghorns. I didn't need anyone to explain the meaning to me.

It was the sound of failure, pure and simple.

Chapter 8

"You flimped," said Chibb. He and the others were standing in a semicircle, looking down at me with sympathetic expressions. I was in exactly the same spot where I'd dropped to the ground at the end of the exercise, legs folded, eyes locked on the grass in front of me.

"Flimped?" said Mr. Beeba. "I'm afraid I'm unfamiliar with the term."

"It's Zarga Baffa jargon, I wouldn't expect you to be," said Chibb. He was making notes in a little notebook. "Flimping is what happens when your fears immobilize you. Akiko flimped when that big fellow over there"—he pointed at the minivan-sized meteor behind him, still sending clouds of smoke up from the

grass—"nearly squashed her." He sighed. "Fortunately she was able to recover, but make no mistake: it was the flimp that cost her the exercise. Without it she'd have made it to the nest just in time."

"Ain't nothin' to be ashamed of, 'Kiko," said Spuckler. "You did good."

"Mmm," said Chibb, neither agreeing nor disagreeing. "Nothing to be proud of, though. Excessive caution, indecision at every turn, and of course a full-blown flimp when the going got tough..." He stopped writing and raised his head. "I've no choice but to give you an A for this lesson, Akiko."

"An *A*?" I said, meeting his gaze for the first time since the exercise ended. It seemed too good to be true.

"For acceptable." He frowned and went back to his note taking. "It's the middle grade in our five-letter scale: F for first-rate, D for distinguished, A for acceptable, P for problematic, and U for unacceptable." He closed his book and tucked it into his robes. "Just be glad I didn't give you an unacceptable. Three U's and your whole team will be rejected from Zarga Baffa, just like the other Smoovian trainees before you."

I wanted to say something in my defense but decided to keep my mouth shut. *It's part of the Zarga Baffa method,* I told myself. *He's just doing this to toughen me up, make me stronger.*

He straightened and clapped his hands twice. "All right. Back to the starting line." He turned and marched across the field. "Let's see if one of you can earn a D this time."

The rest of the morning crawled by. I watched as Gax and Spuckler took their turns, both of them getting the three eggs to the nest in the allotted time. Gax extended three mechanical arms from his body, one for each egg, and dodged the meteors as if he'd been designed especially for it. And Spuckler . . . well, Spuckler was Spuckler: we all expected him to be good at something like this, and he was. (Poog, having no arms or legs, was exempted from the lesson.) When it came time for Mr. Beeba's turn, I confess I crossed my fingers and hoped for him to fail spectacularly. Anything to keep me from being the only one to do poorly.

To the shock of everyone, Mr. Beeba outperformed us all.

"Our first F of the day. Well done!" said Chibb as we left the field and proceeded to the next lesson. "Good heavens, old sport. You had one minute and twenty-two seconds to spare. That may be a record for a being of your height and weight."

"It was all a matter of luck," said Mr. Beeba. "Well, that and the complex series of logarithms I performed in my head prior to the exercise, taking into account the terrain, wind direction, egg weight, and ratio of calories burned to molecules of oxygen inhaled per breath."

"Brilliant," said Chibb, slapping Mr. Beeba on the back. "I can't wait to see how you perform in our next lesson."

Good, I thought. *We're moving on to the next lesson. I've got a chance to redeem myself here. If I do well enough, they'll all forget about this stupid yoodoo bird thing.*

Chapter 9

I'd rather not get into the details of the second lesson of the morning. Basically it involved aquatic robots with jaws like sharks', iron weights shackled to our ankles, and an enormous swimming pool filled with stinky green slime. Needless to say, I didn't volunteer to go first.

Fortunately I wasn't the only one who did poorly this time. Spuckler snapped a jaw off one of the robots by mistake, and the green slime caused Gax to short-circuit about halfway through. Still, when it came to blowing a Zarga Baffa lesson, I was in a class by myself. The weights on my ankles got tangled as soon as I jumped into the pool, and I shot straight to the bottom. The robots came after me, and I totally forgot everything Chibb had said about how best to defend myself against them. After thirty seconds of kicking spastically, flailing my arms, and just generally freaking out, I pushed the panic button we'd each been given at the beginning of the exercise.

When Chibb switched off the robots and fished me out of the slime, I saw that the next group of students—Dregger and his crew—had already come in with their training master, just in time to see my excellent demonstration of how *not* to do it. They were all laughing and pointing at me.

"*Very* impressive," said Dregger, snickering loudly. "But you'd better stick to something your own speed, kiddo. You know, like . . ." He walked over and leaned in close to me, his three beady eyes open wide. ". . . finger painting."

His pals busted up over this one, then turned to me, awaiting a response.

Just ignore him, I told myself. *Putting up a fight is only going to make things worse.*

"Use your head, now, Earthian," said Dregger, strutting away from me as if he'd just slam-dunked a basketball. "You'll think of a good comeback eventually."

"Come along, come along," said Chibb, rushing us out of the room. "Time for lunch. You all need to get something in your stomachs for the afternoon lessons." I'm pretty sure the real reason Chibb was in such a hurry had nothing to do with food and everything to do with his own reputation: my lousy performance reflected badly on him as a training master.

My grade? Chibb gave me a P. In my case it probably stood for pathetic.

Lunch was the nastiest thing I'd ever seen anyone dare to dump on a plate. Calling it food was some kind of sick joke. It was cold, pinkish gray, and coiled tightly in on itself like a small intestine. It smelled like something scraped off the bottom of a fish tank. I didn't want to put so much as a *sliver* of this thing in my mouth.

So I didn't. I just sat there staring at the walls of

the drafty, dark room off the cafeteria where all the
Humbling Week students were forced to eat. It was
a dreary place, but it had one distinct advantage: it
was free of Chibb Fallaby, who had left us there so
that he could eat with the other training masters.

"Gotta eat sometime, 'Kiko," said Spuckler,
thick gray liquid dripping from his nose and lips.
"That roll you munched for breakfast ain't even
gonna take ya halfway through the afternoon. You'll
wind up so tuckered out you'll faint dead away."

I knew Spuckler was right. And I was *seriously*
hungry, there was no denying it. But I was determined to skip lunch anyway. Part of it was the gross-
out factor of the food, of course. But there was

something else. A weird sinking feeling inside me. The lousy grades I'd got, the things Chibb had said to me, the cold, wet hole that was waiting for me at the end of the day . . . it was all coming together and pushing down on me like a big, heavy rock.

"Do you think it's possible for us to switch training masters?" I asked anyone who cared to answer.

Mr. Beeba swallowed noisily and adjusted his spectacles. "Good heavens, Akiko. Don't tell me you're dissatisfied with Master Fallaby. I think he's been doing an exemplary job."

"Yeah, well, I'm not so sure about that," I said. "Did you hear him call me 'child'? Who does he think he is? I'll bet he's no more than five years older than I am, if that."

"I CERTAINLY SYMPATHIZE WITH YOUR FEELINGS, MA'AM," said Gax. "BUT YOU MUSTN'T FORGET THAT THIS IS HUMBLING WEEK. MASTER FALLABY'S WORDS ARE NO DOUBT CALCULATED TO PRESS YOU ONWARD TO GREATER ACHIEVEMENTS."

"Absolutely," said Mr. Beeba. "It's all part of the

Zarga Baffa method. It's nothing personal. He's stoking the fires of your determination to succeed. A very clever tactic, really, if you step back and take a good look at it."

I thought this over. Gax and Mr. Beeba were probably right. Maybe if I really gave my all in the next lesson and showed everyone how serious I was about becoming a space patroller, Chibb would let up on me a little. Besides, it wasn't Chibb I needed to focus on, but King Froptoppit and everyone else back on the planet Smoo. They were counting on us to graduate, and if that meant putting up with Chibb Fallaby, then I'd just have to learn to live with the guy.

"Well, one thing's for sure. I've got nowhere to go from here but up."

"You're doin' fine, 'Kiko," said Spuckler. "You'll be the best patroller this camp ever saw, jus' you wait an' see."

I smiled at Spuckler. Things weren't so bad, really. Maybe they were about to get better.

Chapter 10

The afternoon lessons started out pretty well. Chibb led us to an outdoor section of the training camp that looked like a scale model of the Grand Canyon. We had to practice riding these six-legged lizards called nognags, which were as big as cows and just as slow-moving. They had black and orange skin and long, pointy anteater snouts.

There were reasons to be optimistic. My parents had allowed me to take riding lessons at camp a couple of summers earlier, so I already had some experience. The teacher had even said I was a natural. Of course, a horse and a six-legged lizard are two very different things, but even so, I felt I had a head start on this one.

Chibb taught us four words before he let us get in the saddle: *k-chooka,* which made the animals go faster; *whup-whup,* which made them go slower; *sh-zilla,* which made them jump; and *pastabak,* which made them come to a complete stop. I had the words pretty well memorized as we made our way onto the path we'd be following for the duration of the exercise: a narrow dusty trail that led through a series of ravines and gullies designed to test our riding skills.

"*K-chikka!*" yelled Spuckler, trying to get his nognag to pick up the pace. "I said *k-chikka,* ya dagnabbed slowpoke. What are ya, stone deaf?"

"It's *k-chooka,* Spuckler," I said, smiling. *Finally, something I'm good at.*

"Thanks, 'Kiko," said Spuckler before bellowing into his nognag's ears: "*K-chooka! K-CHOOOOOOOO-KAAAAA!*" The half-asleep beast shuddered irritably, began moving slightly faster for a moment, then resumed his original slow lope.

"Aw, for cryin' out loud," moaned Spuckler. "This

here nognag's the slowest beast a burden in the whole goldurned galaxy!"

"But of course, Spuckler," said Chibb from his own nognag, bringing up the rear of our little troop. "I deliberately put you on old Swappy there for that very reason: to test your patience. It's just what you need to round out your adventuring abilities."

So Chibb paired us with different nognags depending on what we needed to learn. Maybe there's something to this Zarga Baffa method after all.

The nognags carried us around a bend and down to a gently babbling brook.

"We're going to cross this stream one at a time," called Chibb. "Nognags have a strong aversion to water. The only way to get through is to increase speed until they're forced across by their own momentum."

I watched as Spuckler, Gax, Mr. Beeba, and Poog guided their nognags through the water with varying degrees of success. The riverbed was muddy, and the nognags howled in protest, but everyone made it to the other side in one piece. It looked tricky but doable.

"Your turn, Akiko," Chibb said from behind me. I turned and saw a trace of a smile on his lips.

I'll start with a couple of k-chookas *and maybe throw in a* sh-zilla *or two if I get stuck.*

I patted my nognag and whispered in its ear. "Help me out here, big guy. I've already blown two lessons today. Get me across this river and I'll . . ." I took the reins in my hands and gripped them as hard as I could. ". . . I don't know, give you an apple or something."

I took one last peek at Chibb, then turned and focused on the stream. I took a deep breath and said loudly and clearly, *"K-chooka!"*

I saw a flash of red somewhere off to my left—very small, but very bright. A split second later—*whoosh!*—my nognag took off so quickly I thought it must have sprouted wings.

Water exploded all over me as we plunged into the stream and tore across it in a split second. We barreled out of the water like a rocket, sending stones and pebbles flying in all directions. I caught a blurry glimpse of Spuckler and Mr. Beeba diving off their nognags to get out of our path.

Chibb cried something—for the life of me, I have no idea what—as the nognag charged up over a hill and carried me away.

A lunatic lizard! was all I could think as the nognag left the trail altogether and galloped into an impossibly narrow ravine. *Chibb put me on a lunatic lizard!*

Rocks. Sky. Clouds of dust. There was no making sense of what we were doing or where we were going. I just held on to the reins for dear life and hoped we wouldn't smash straight into a wall of stone.

The nognag howled like a wolf as it leaped off the side of a good-sized cliff. I stared in horror at the ground, fully sixty feet below, nothing but air between it and me.

Fifty feet.

Forty.

Thirty.

Twenty.

Ten.

FWAM!

The nognag struck the ground and shot back off it like a ricocheting bullet.

All right, that does it. I'm letting go.

I shut my eyes and released my grip on the reins.

"Yyyyyaaarrrrgh!"

The sensation of burning on my wrists was unbearable. My arms were entangled with the reins. Like it or not, I was attached to this nognag for the duration.

The word for "stop"! What's the word for "stop"?

Normally I had a very good short-term memory. But with the reins burning into my wrists and my body flipping back and forth like a hooked fish, it was impossible to concentrate long enough to recall the word I needed.

The nognag was now hurtling through a field of towering cactuslike plants, clearing them by mere inches on either side. Needles grazed my arms and shoulders, sending stabs of pain through my entire body.

Paster-something.

"Pasternak!"

Nope. The nognag seemed—if anything—to be *gathering* speed as it reached the edge of the riding range, leaped a fence, and tore off into an entirely different part of the training complex. Within seconds we were charging straight into a playing field where advanced trainees were in the middle of a game that looked something like lacrosse.

Pasta. It was Pasta something.

"Pasta pack!"

Trainees, shouting their dismay, leaped out of the way as we sped across the field and crashed through a row of bleachers, sending a group of one-eyed aliens flying through the air. Angry cries echoed behind me as the nognag cut through a gigantic hangar full of astroshuttles, hung left, then set its sights on one of the glass domes on the edge of the Zarga Baffa complex.

No! Not through the glass!

There was only one hope: I had to remember the stop word, and it had to be now.

"*Pasta whack! Pasta jack! Pasta shack! Pasta plaque!*"

The nognag jumped a row of tall hedges, the only thing left to keep it from plowing into the side of the dome.

"*Pasta knack! Pasta flack! Past a stack! Passed a snack!*"

I had only seconds left. It was now or never.

"*Pastabak!*"

It was the right word. I knew it. And if the nognag had actually *heard* it, we would have stopped just in time. But the lizard was so out of control by this point I might as well have shouted "Abracadabra" into its ear for all the good it did.

I closed my eyes as the nognag leaped and soared through the air toward the huge sheet of glass before us.

CRRRRAAAAAAAAAAASSSSHHHH!

A tornado of glass shards whirled around us as we blasted through the dome and careened into the room beyond. Startled cries erupted on all sides as I felt myself slide across the floor into something cold, wet, and sticky. When I raised my head I found myself still attached to the reins of the nognag (which had belatedly come to a complete stop) and covered head to toe with meat, vegetables, and a substance that looked and smelled like lemon meringue pie.

I had ridden the nognag straight into the Zarga Baffa cafeteria.

Chapter 11

"**No broken b-bones.** No torn ligaments. Just bruises and mild abrasions. You're a lucky g-girl."

A multiarmed alien doctor was examining me in the Zarga Baffa medical clinic. She had little purple eyes on all sides of her furry head, two incredibly long antennae, and an extremely bad case of dandruff.

"*Very* lucky," said Chibb. He was in the clinic with me. Spuckler and the others were waiting outside. My spectacular mishap with the nognag had softened his attitude toward me a bit, and he had almost turned back into the kind, caring Chibb he'd been when I first met him.

"A few more b-bandages and she'll be free to go," said the doctor. "I'll be right b-back."

"Thanks for patching her up, Zaydia," he said as the doctor slithered from the room. "Just send her to one of the recuperation rooms when you're done. We'll give her the rest of the day off and have her make up the remainder of today's lessons some other time. Speaking of which," he said to me after the doctor was gone, "I'd better get back to the others. Don't worry, Akiko, you'll be in good hands here."

"Chibb," I said.

"Yes?"

"Why did you put me on that nognag?"

Chibb looked startled by my question. He stared at me for a long time before answering.

"That nognag was suffering from a nervous disorder, Akiko: bi-thalamacular nogatosis. I assure you I had no way of knowing that when I assigned her to you. We try to make sure all our nognags are fit and healthy, but every once in a while a bad one slips through." He paused and added: "Please accept my apologies." He said it more as a command than a request.

I think I was supposed to say "That's okay" or "Don't worry about it," but I couldn't bring myself to say either of those things. What I did say was this: "So what grade are you going to give me?"

"Why, a U, of course."

"A *U*?" I couldn't believe it. "Unacceptable? You can't *do* that!"

"I can and *must* do it, Akiko." His face was hard and drained of emotion. "Good nognag or bad, you should have remembered the words for controlling it. Forgetting them resulted in *unprecedented* damage to Zarga Baffa property, and put *dozens* of innocent trainees in harm's way."

I was speechless with anger. Tears welled up in my eyes, but I couldn't bear to let Chibb see me cry. So I choked them back and just sat there on the examination table, staring at my bandaged wrists.

"Attitude is everything on Zarga Baffa, Akiko.

And yours," Chibb said before turning his back to me, "needs a little work."

k-chak

He closed the door, leaving me alone.

"If ever you find yourself troubled by any aspect of your training," Odo Mumzibar had said when we first arrived, "please feel free to come directly to me." Well, I was now officially troubled with my training, that's for sure.

After an hour or so in one of the recuperation rooms, I decided to pay Odo Mumzibar a quick visit and see if he agreed with me that Chibb's grade was unfair. I asked one of the nurses how to get to Head-master Mumzibar's office. She drew me a map and said, "When you see the umbrellas, take the sturdi-est one you can find." She smiled and added: "Unless you like getting wet."

I followed her directions to a path leading off to the edge of the Zarga Baffa complex. The path twisted and turned through a shadowy green forest.

The air was misty and damp and smelled of woodsmoke. I began to hear the sound of a waterfall in the distance. The farther I walked, the louder the sound grew, until I knew I was walking straight toward it. Finally I came to a clearing and, sure enough, found myself standing directly in front of a waterfall, which was pouring down from a steep cliff of tall, moss-covered rocks. The path on which I had been walking led to a small stone bridge that went right into the middle of the waterfall.

I looked at the map the nurse had drawn for me. To get to Odo Mumzibar's quarters, I would have to cross the bridge and go straight through the water.

These Zarga Baffa guys, I thought. *They love to make things difficult.*

To my right was a rough wooden barrel with a half dozen umbrellas in it. I grabbed the sturdiest one I could find—a rickety little thing that looked as if it was made of sticks and straw—took a deep breath, and had one last look at the barrier before me. It was only water, but man, it was thundering down onto that bridge like Niagara Falls. Raising the umbrella over my head and praying it wouldn't get pounded to pieces, I dashed full speed into the water.

It took a few seconds to get to the other side, and I ended up sopping wet. There was a gap of about five feet between the water and the cliff wall behind it. At the point where the bridge met the cliff was a small wooden door with a rusty iron ring attached in the middle. I took the iron ring in my hand and knocked it against the door three times.

After half a minute or so the door opened, all by itself.

"Come in," said the voice of Odo Mumzibar. "Come in and dry yourself by the fire."

I stepped through the doorway and the door creaked shut behind me. I was in a small, round room with rough stone walls. It was little more than a cave, hacked out of the side of the cliff with simple tools and an awful lot of hard work. There was very little furniture, just a writing table and a pair of sturdy bookshelves.

In the middle of the room was a shallow pit holding a crackling fire. A blackened hole in the ceiling carried most of the smoke away, but the room still smelled like a campground. On the other side of the fire, seated upon a big, flat stone, was Odo Mumzibar.

"Sit, dear girl," he said. "Sit down at my side." I nodded and—since there was no chair—planted myself directly on the floor. The warmth of the fire was wonderful, but I was too nervous to enjoy it very much. I felt as if I were seated next to a mighty sorcerer or a high priest.

Odo Mumzibar peered into my eyes, sizing me up. For a minute I wondered if he was trying to read my mind.

We both sat there in silence for a moment. Then Odo Mumzibar took hold of a wooden box in front of him, opened it, and produced a small ceramic sphere. It was half black, half red, and covered with tiny alien carvings. It looked like an artifact from a museum, possibly an object used in some strange ancient ritual. He handed it to me.

"Before you speak," he said, "you must do as I say."

I swallowed hard and nodded.

It's some kind of a test. If I pass, he'll allow me to talk. And if I fail?

I swallowed again.

Better not fail.

"Take the black half in your right hand and the red half in your left hand."

I did as I was told.

"Hold the black half steady. Turn the red half away."

Again, I did as I was told. Or *tried* to, anyway. The

two halves of the sphere seemed permanently joined, as if they had been designed not to turn at all.

"Be strong, be true," whispered Odo Mumzibar, his eyes burning into mine. "Hold fast, and focus with the whole of your mind, the whole of your spirit."

I pressed my fingers against the sphere as hard as I could and tried with all my might to turn the two halves in opposite directions. They wouldn't budge.

"Close your eyes," whispered Odo Mumzibar. "Put everything you have into the task at hand."

I shut my eyes and tensed every muscle in my body.

"*Feel* it giving way. *See* it giving way in your mind, and it shall be so!"

I clenched my teeth and gave it my all. I growled and shook like a wild animal.

"Yes! That's it! Draw upon the power within!"

"*Nnnnnngh-aaaaaaaarrrrggh!*"

With a triumphant shout—a hoarse bellow of a cry that I didn't realize I was capable of making—

I twisted the two halves away from one another and felt them turn in my hands, gliding freely at last, as if they'd never been stuck together in the first place.

"Good, *good,*" said Odo Mumzibar, his eyes crinkling with approval. "I knew you could do it." He unfolded his wrinkled fingers and stretched them out before my face. "Now put it into my hands."

Panting, exhausted, but deeply relieved, I gave the sphere back to Odo Mumzibar. He took it in his hands and continued turning the two halves, rotating them again and again and again. Finally they separated altogether, and I saw that one side was filled with a dollop of pinkish gray goo. Poking a finger into it, Odo Mumzibar took a taste of it.

"Mmmm," he said, "Libbling jelly. A gift from my aunt P'foomia." He reached into the wooden box and pulled out a plateful of crackers and a small butter knife. "Lovely stuff, though one does wish they wouldn't make the jars so *devilishly* hard to open."

He dipped the knife into the goo, put a generous smear on one of the crackers, and handed it to me. "Now then, my dear child, what brings you here to visit me?" Within seconds he had covered a second cracker with jelly and popped it into his mouth. Chewing noisily, looking surprisingly like a horse with a mouthful of hay, he blinked and waited for a reply. "Hm?"

"Um." I cleared my throat and tried to collect my thoughts. "It's, uh, it's about my training master."

"Ah, Chibb," said Odo Mumzibar, already preparing another cracker. "Splendid fellow. One of the best we've got. What about him?"

"He gave me a U today."

Odo Mumzibar nodded. "Mm. Unacceptable. Yes, it's terrible to get one of those, isn't it? Got *two* of them back when I was a trainee." He stared me in the eye. "Are you questioning Master Fallaby's judgment, then?"

"Oh, no," I said. "Not really." I coughed. "Well,

yes, actually." I leaned forward and searched Odo Mumzibar's face for signs of sympathy. "Um . . . *maybe?*"

Odo Mumzibar took another bite and chewed thoughtfully. "Tell me what happened."

I took a deep breath and told Odo about the nognag lesson, and all the crazy stuff that had happened, and how it wasn't my fault that I'd wound up going straight into the Zarga Baffa cafeteria. When I was done I stopped talking and waited for his reaction, hoping he'd agree that under the circumstances I deserved better than a U.

"A highly unusual situation," Odo Mumzibar said at last. "It's been years since we've had a bad nognag slip through like that. Please accept my apologies." I shuddered, realizing that Chibb had said the exact same thing, though in a much less kindly way. "Still, you did forget the command, didn't you?"

I nodded and said, "Yes," so quietly even *I* could barely hear me.

"I understand how you feel, dear girl. I will keep

a close eye on your progress here from now on. But for the moment I must let Master Fallaby's judgment stand." He popped the last of a cracker in his mouth and swallowed it. "Let the U do what it does best: stir up your fighting spirit, steel your resolve to do better. I've seen enough today to know that when you put your mind to it"—he pointed at the two halves of the ceramic sphere and gave me a knowing look—"you are capable of great things."

I smiled in spite of myself. Though Odo Mumzibar hadn't taken my side, he had somehow made me feel better.

"Now, eat that cracker, my child," he added with a mischievous grin, "or I'll eat it for you."

Chapter 12

I left Odo Mumzibar's quarters and returned to the recuperation room. At the end of the day I joined Spuckler and the others for the long walk back to the holes. I told them about my visit to Odo Mumzibar and the bad grade that had prompted it.

"A U?" said Spuckler. "That ain't right. That ain't even *close* to right."

"It does seem a bit extreme," said Mr. Beeba. "But again, you must think of these things within the context of the Zarga Baffa method. Odo Mumzibar is quite right. The poor grades are calculated to make you work harder."

"Maybe," I said. "But what if I get two more U's?

Then our whole team will be sent home, and King Froptoppit will know that I was the one who messed everything up."

"YOU WON'T GET ANY MORE U'S, MA'AM," said Gax with a rattle of his helmet. "I'M SURE OF IT. YOU'LL IMPROVE, AND CHIBB WILL GIVE YOU BETTER AND BETTER GRADES. YOU'LL BE ONE OF THE GREATEST GRADUATES ZARGA BAFFA HAS EVER SEEN."

Poog nodded and added a few gurgly, gargled words.

"Poog agrees," said Mr. Beeba. "He sees great rewards awaiting you at the end of all this."

I gave Poog the best smile I could manage. "Thanks, Poog. I hope you're right. I really do."

I had thought that my injuries would exempt me from climbing the giant muddy hill, but I should have known better. Humbling Week was all about pain, and if you felt more of it than everyone else, so much the better.

Spuckler and Mr. Beeba went first, while Gax and Poog stayed with me as I slowly slogged up the slope, trying my best not to incur any further scrapes from the jagged stones. I was about halfway up the hill when I heard a voice behind me.

"Hey, look, it's the maniac nognag rider!"

I didn't even have to turn around to know it was Dregger: I recognized his nasal voice.

"Didja see what she did to the cafeteria? I can't believe she didn't get expelled for that. They prob'ly cut her some slack 'cause she's a puny little Earthian."

I gotta just ignore him. Pretend he's not even there.

"Hey, Noggy!" He was closer now, just a few yards away. "How was the food? I hear you went from the appetizer to the dessert in under a second!" His laughter echoed across the hill and was joined by several alien chuckles: the other members of his crew.

Poog, Gax, and I finally reached the top of the hill, but old long-arms was right behind us.

"So is it true Fallaby socked ya with a U for that?" He stuck his face in front of me and stared gleefully with all three of his eyes. "Two more of those and it's buh-bye to you and all your buddies here!"

I couldn't take it anymore.

"What planet are you from?" I stuck my face so close to his we could smell each other's breath. (I got the worse part of the bargain, no question.)

Dregger was a little startled by my question, as though a response from me was against the rules of his little game.

"Plaptoll," he said. "What about it?"

"Earthians eat Plaptollian arms for breakfast, you know," I said to him. "We turn them into sausage. Fry them in oil."

He looked truly horrified for a moment, then laughed nervously. "She's a joker, guys," he said, turning back to the other members of his group. "We got ourselves a joker here!" He stopped following me, though, and that was the last I heard out of him for the evening.

By the time I'd waded through the swamp and crawled into my hole, I thought I'd be asleep within seconds. There was one thing keeping me awake, though: hunger, hunger like I'd never felt in my life. Skipping dinner the previous night had been a mistake. Skipping lunch . . . well, that had been an act of sheer insanity. When Grunn Grung arrived with my evening bucket of slop, I grabbed it from him and started wolfing it down without even pausing to look at it.

"Seeeeee?" said Grunn Grung. "You eeeaaat. You eeeaaaat."

I don't even want to say what it tasted like: moldy cheese, stewed pig livers . . . nothing's quite disgusting enough to make a good comparison. But who cares? It was food. I ate every last morsel of it and licked the sides of the bucket clean. I'd have licked the bottom but my tongue wasn't long enough.

"Goooooooood," said Grunn Grung when he returned to collect the bucket. "Noooow . . . you sleeeeeeep."

I fell back and rested my head on the cold, wet stones.

My first day, I thought. *This was just my first day. I've got six more to go.*

I closed my eyes.

I'm never going to make it.

Chapter 13

"Wake up."

Someone was tapping me on the shoulder. I opened my eyes. It was still pitch black out, well before dawn. Alien crickets and toads chirped and croaked, but otherwise it was dead quiet.

"Come on, Earthian," the voice whispered, accompanied by several more taps on my shoulder. "Wake up already."

I turned over and found the little red-suited alien, helmet off, arms around her knees, sitting just inside the entrance to my hole. Who knew how long she'd been there?

"What are you—"

"Shhhhhh." She put a tiny finger to her little pink lips. There was just enough moonlight to make out the details of her face: pointy nose, oversized ears, little green stripes on her chin and forehead. "Keep it down. People are sleeping."

Yeah, I thought, *like me until a few seconds ago.*

"Okay," I whispered, rubbing my eyes. "What are you doing here? And while we're at it, who *are* you?"

"I'm Raspa-Nanga Leely Kayooli." She lowered her eyes and bowed politely. "You can call me Raspa."

"Raspa," I said, relieved that I wouldn't have to memorize all those other names. "I'm Aki—"

"Akiko. I know, I know. You're already famous here. You don't ride a nognag into the middle of the Zarga Baffa cafeteria without your name getting around."

"All right, so you know my name. I'm assuming you didn't sneak up here in the middle of the night just to prove that to me."

"Hey, a little less attitude and a little more gratitude. I'm taking a big risk here for your benefit."

"Okay, okay. What's this all about?"

She turned away from me, poked her head out of the hole, and took a good look in all directions. "It's about . . ." She turned back to face me, concern in her piercing little eyes. "It's about me trying to clue you in. Because, let's face it, you don't have a clue what's going on, do you?"

"Clue about what?"

"Clue about Chibb Fallaby," she said. "About why he's making things hard for you." She followed this with a nod and a knowing arch of the eyebrows.

"Well, go on. I'm listening."

"Chibb Fallaby hates Earthians. Hates your whole home planet."

"No way. Really?"

"With a passion."

"But . . . why?"

She paused and ran a hand through her spiky green hair. "I'll keep this as short as possible. Chibb's got an older brother. Nool Fallaby. You know that name?"

"No."

She rolled her eyes, as if I were even more clueless than she'd first imagined.

"Okay, well, Nool Fallaby used to be an intergalactic explorer, one of the best Zarga Baffa ever had. He once visited Earth, back when Chibb was still just a kid. It was a matter of great family pride.

Nool was the first Zarga Baffian to visit all the populated planets of the Milky Way."

"So what happened when he got to Earth? He didn't like it there?"

"Oh, he *loved* it there. Stayed on Earth longer than any of the other planets. It was after he came back to Zarga Baffa that the troubles began. See, he picked something up on Earth."

"Picked something up?"

"An illness. I think you Earthians call it the flow: fever, chills, muscular pain."

"The *flow*?"

"Don't tell me you've never heard of it. It's very common on your planet."

I thought for a moment. Then it hit me.

"The *flu*," I said. "You're talking about the *flu*, not the flow."

"Flu, flow, whatever. The thing is, once Chibb's brother got this thing, he was never able to shake it. The finest medical minds in all of Zarga Baffa tried to help him, but nothing could be done.

It pretty much ended his career as an explorer. Really wrecked the guy. And, more importantly—from *your* point of view—it affected Chibb in a big way."

"Why, did Chibb catch the flu from his brother?"

"No, no, no." Raspa shook her head crisply. "The doctors made sure of that. Kept Nool quarantined. Confined him to a wing of the Zarga Baffa hospital for years. Think about it: here was this guy that Chibb looked up to—a real hero to him—reduced to coughing and wheezing for the rest of his life. And all because of your home planet."

I thought about what she was saying. Chibb *had* made a point of saying that I was the first Earthian ever to attend the Zarga Baffa training camp, so he was certainly aware of my origins.

"So you think Chibb blames *me* for his brother getting sick."

"I'm not saying that. All I'm saying is that when Chibb sees you, he thinks about Earth. And when he thinks about Earth, he gets angry."

"So you think he stuck me with that crazy nog-nag on purpose?"

"Who knows? It's a pretty weird coincidence, though." She rose to leave. "*Really* weird, if you ask me."

"Wait a minute," I said. "You can't leave yet. You've got to tell me what to do."

She was already halfway out of the hole, but she stopped long enough to say one more thing: "I can't live your life for you, Akiko. You make your own decisions. But if I were you, I'd cry blue and hop the next astroshuttle out of here. Because this I know for sure: Chibb Fallaby will grow wings and hoot like a yoodoo bird before he allows an Earthian to graduate from this training camp. That's all there is to it. And believe you me," she added, her eyes tensing into a fierce squint, "if you think Chibb has been tough on you so far, you ain't seen nothin' yet."

With that she leaped into the air and disappeared from view. I poked my head out to follow her descent, but she moved so quickly, all I caught was a flash of red as she vanished into her hole. All at once everything was as it had been before: alien crickets chirping, gray moonlit haze drifting through the trees.

Raspa's words echoed in my head: "All I'm saying is that when Chibb sees you, he thinks about Earth. And when he thinks about Earth, he gets angry."

Is she right about all that? Is Chibb really out to get me?

There was certainly no shortage of evidence to back her up. The meteor that came within a hair of landing on me. The angry edge to Chibb's voice every time he talked to me. And the nognag he stuck me with, the one that turned me into the laughingstock of Zarga Baffa. The more I thought about it, the more frightened I became of what lay ahead.

Okay, suppose Chibb really does have something against me graduating, I thought. *If he does, he's going to give me two more U's. Then our whole team will be sent home.*

But if I cry blue like Raspa says, I'm the only one who will get sent home. Spuckler, Gax, Mr. Beeba, and Poog will at least have a chance.

What a decision! Crying blue was the last thing I wanted to do. But if Chibb really did have an anti-Earthian bias, having me around was going to ruin things for the others.

I tossed and turned, trying to figure out what was the best thing to do.

I don't want to be a quitter, I thought before closing my eyes for a few more hours of fitful sleep, *but this time I may have no choice.*

Chapter 14

The second day of lessons was no better than the first. After giving us another bitter black lump for breakfast, Chibb led us to a dark and drafty gymnasium for a series of robo-alien wrestling exercises.

"Oh yeah, this is gonna be a hoot," said Spuckler, giddy with anticipation as we found our seats beside a large octagonal ring. "Can't wait to treat one of these fellers to my backhand half nelson." The mat was scuff-marked, dusty, and covered with stains (many of which, I had no doubt, were the blood and body fluids of earlier trainees).

"We'll start with the bipeds and quadrupeds," said Chibb, "then work our way up to the decapeds and gazoolapeds." He began passing around leather kneepads and sweat-stained headgear. "Make sure you keep these guards clamped tightly across your foreheads. Some of these guys know a move that'll make your eyes pop out of their sockets."

I was watching Chibb in a whole new way now, analyzing him for evidence of an anti-Earthian bias. If he had one, he was good at hiding it. He treated me pretty much like the others. But I couldn't help wondering if Raspa was right. Was Chibb somehow stacking the deck against me?

I'll wait and see if he gives me another U, I thought. *If he doesn't, then there's no need to cry blue. But if he does . . .*

The robo-alien wrestling was exhausting, painful, and—at times—highly embarrassing. I held my own against my first opponent, Uklay, a slow-moving beast with seven-clawed hands and a long, crooked tail. The second one, though—a potbellied, spiky-backed creature named Lulk—wore me out within minutes. I tried all the evasive moves Chibb taught us at the outset of the lesson: leaping and cartwheeling over the beast's shoulders, ducking and somersaulting between his legs. But it was no use. I ended up pinned to the mat with my head between my legs, my arms locked behind my back, and my butt sticking straight up in the air.

"Come on, child, fight!" cried Chibb as the staticky voice of the robo-alien counted down from twenty to zero. "Show me what you're made of!"

Whatever I was made of, it clearly wasn't good robo-wrestling material. Lulk beat me handily. My third and final match (against a long-legged freaky thing that hissed and banged like a broken washing machine) was over in a matter of seconds.

Chibb shut the robo-alien off and pulled me out from underneath it. He was disappointed. Worse than that: he was angry.

"There's a problem with your motivation today, Akiko. You seem confused, indecisive. Anything you need to talk about with me?"

Maybe I should ask him about what Raspa said. Find out if it's true.

"Are you . . . ," I began, then stopped myself. I wasn't sure how to put the question.

"Am I what?"

Even if it's true, he's not going to admit it. It's not going to do me any good to put him on the spot like this.

"Are you . . . going to give me an A or a P?"

Chibb shook his head. "Oh, is that it? The grades. Is that all you care about, Akiko? Getting an A or a P?"

"No," I said, "but—"

"This is *not* about grades, Akiko," Chibb said, his face hardening. "This is about doing your very best. Giving your all. And you, child, are not giving your all. You're not even giving your *half*."

"I'm *trying*," I said. "I really am."

"Well, here's something to make you try harder, Akiko," Chibb said. "Another U."

My heart began pounding. Blood rushed to my face.

Raspa's right. He's giving me U's on purpose. He's against me. He is!

"You hate me," I said, startled by the sound of the words coming from my own mouth. "You hate me because I'm an Earthian!"

Mr. Beeba and Poog stared at me in disbelief. Gax cocked his head to one side, maybe thinking he'd misheard me. Even Spuckler—who was in the middle of a furious series of stretching exercises in preparation for his first match—looked surprised.

But no one looked more stunned than Chibb. Was he shocked because I'd discovered his secret? Or was he simply unaware of the fact that he'd been treating me unfairly? It was impossible to tell.

"Enough," he said after a very long silence. "Go to the bench and cool off, Akiko. We'll resume this discussion when you are in a more reasonable state of mind."

At lunch it didn't take long for everyone to start asking about my outburst. I told them all about Raspa and the secret information she'd shared with me in the middle of the night. I pointed out all the evidence. Then I told them how crying blue was the only way I could save everyone's chances of graduating.

"I don't know, 'Kiko," said Spuckler between mouthfuls of gray-green sludge. "I mean, you've had a pretty rough time of it, sure. But Chibb bein' out to getcha just 'cause you're an Earthian? Sounds a little far-fetched."

"Normally I try not to do this," said Mr. Beeba, "but I'm going to have to agree with Spuckler. I'll attest to the fact that Chibb has been pushing you, and pushing you hard, but the idea that he is deliberately trying to stop you from graduating strikes me as improbable at best."

"What about the nognag?" I said. "How do you explain that?"

"IT WAS A MOST UNFORTUNATE TURN OF EVENTS, MA'AM," said Gax, "BUT WELL WITHIN THE REALM OF STATISTICAL COINCIDENCE. INDEED, AS I RECALL, MASTER FALLABY NEARLY ASSIGNED THAT NOGNAG TO ME, BUT CHANGED HIS MIND WHEN HE SAW THAT ITS BACK WAS NOT BROAD ENOUGH TO SUPPORT MY AXLES."

I turned to Poog, gesturing at him with out-stretched palms. "What do you think, Poog? You've been watching Chibb. All this stuff is more than just coincidence. It's got to be."

Poog paused before answering. I could see my own pleading expression reflected in his big, glassy eyes.

Poog frowned, then quietly uttered a few warbly syllables in Toogolian. Mr. Beeba nodded as he prepared to translate. "Poog says there is merit to both sides of the argument. He says you are right about Chibb in certain respects and wrong about him in others."

"Okay, then I'm at least half right." I held my breath and tried to swallow a bite of food so quickly that I wouldn't actually taste it. "Anyway, the point is I need to cry blue. I don't want to, but I *have* to. Otherwise, Chibb's going to give me another U, and then none of us will graduate."

"It is *far* from a foregone conclusion," said Mr. Beeba, "that Chibb is going to give you another U,

Akiko. He's trying to motivate you, that's all. He's put you into this position because he knows that you will do your best when the stakes are highest."

"Ya can't cry blue, 'Kiko," said Spuckler. "It ain't in your blood. You're a fighter, not a quitter."

"I know that, but what else can I do? I'm dealing with a guy who's out to get me!"

Just then, from directly behind my head: "Out to get you? Who's out to get you?"

I turned my head to find Chibb Fallaby standing right next to me. I swallowed so hard I thought I would choke.

"Well? Come on," he said. "Tell me. As your training master, I'd really like to know."

"I . . . I'm not sure."

Chibb smiled, but his eyebrows were drawn together knowingly. He leaned over and put a hand on my shoulder, sending a chill straight down my spine. "Well, if you find out, be sure to let me know. I don't want anyone tormenting my students. Especially Zarga Baffa's very first Earthian."

I opened my mouth, but no words came out.

"All right," said Chibb, straightening up and clapping his hands together. "Lunchtime's over. Off to our afternoon lessons."

Chapter 15

The afternoon lessons—the last I'd have to suffer through, I told myself—looked to be relatively simple. Chibb led us to a darkened room where a replica of a rocket ship was suspended in midair by a network of pulleys and cables. It was a pretty small rocket ship, about the size of a bus, and different from a real rocket ship in that there were no markings of exhaust smoke on the rear boosters. The midsection of the ship was covered with a wide band of reinforced steel. There were indentations all over it, as if something had slammed into it many thousands of times.

Chibb opened the cockpit door and spent a good half hour showing us how to fly it. Luckily for me it wasn't all that different from *Boach's Bullet,* the ship I'd flown in the Alpha Centauri 5000, so I already had a pretty good idea of what I'd need to do once I got behind the controls.

"The purpose of this exercise is to test your powers of concentration," said Chibb as he handed around metallic gray boxes, one for each of us. "Any fool can pilot a rocket ship. But only a Zarga Baffa graduate can pilot a rocket ship *and* make a muzzle-gup sandwich at the same time."

A sandwich? What is this, some kind of joke?

I opened my box. It contained two slices of olive green bread, a hunk of yellow meat, an assortment of brightly colored vegetables, several jars of condiments, and a stubby little knife.

"Instructions on how to make a proper muzzle-gup sandwich are printed on the inside of the lid," said Chibb. "Study them carefully. I'll be inspecting your sandwiches at the conclusion of the exercise. Points will be deducted for meat sliced too thickly—an eighth inch *means* an eighth inch—and condiments oozing off the edges of the bread will bring you down a full grade. Don't even *think* about applying the veggies in the wrong order."

By the tone of Chibb's voice, you'd have thought he was talking about triple bypass surgery. Making a sandwich while flying a rocket ship—silly as it sounded to me—was clearly a matter of grave importance to him. "Any questions?"

Spuckler raised his hand. "Do we get t' eat the sammiches when we're done?"

Chibb grinned. "I'll tell you what, Spuckler. If everyone gets at least a D, you will be rewarded with the sandwiches. Otherwise they go to the training master, as is the custom."

I had just one question, but I wasn't about to ask it: *Should I cry blue as soon as the exercise begins, or wait until I've goofed around with this stupid sandwich first?*

Better wait until about halfway through, I told myself. *Don't want to make it too obvious I planned to quit from the start.*

"It's been a while since you went first, Akiko," said Chibb. "Why don't you get in there and show us how it's done?"

I studied his face. Did he know about my plan to cry blue? Impossible. How could he?

"Okay," I said. Tucking the metallic lunchbox under my arm, I climbed the small stairway that led to the door of the rocket ship.

I shut the door and strapped myself in. The cockpit was small and dark, and stank from the sweat of hundreds of alien trainees. (I thought *human* perspiration smelled bad, but believe me, it's like honeysuckle compared to some of the nose-bendingly stinky sweat out there in the universe.)

"Don't open the box until you see the green light on the dashboard!" said Chibb from his position behind a bank of levers about a hundred feet from the nose of the rocket ship. "All right. Here we go."

BVVVVVvvvvvvvv

The rocket hummed and rose into the air. I could hear the movements of the cables and pulleys, but the illusion of flight was still pretty convincing. Chibb yanked a lever and the rocket began to bank to the right.

VVVVVRRRrrrrrrrrrr

My seat vibrated so strongly that I could barely see straight. The challenge of making a sandwich under these conditions was becoming crystal clear.

TING

A large bulb on the dashboard glowed bright green as the rocket began to roll back to a more even keel.

I shouldn't even bother, I thought as I opened the metallic box in my lap, *but what the heck?* I couldn't bring myself to admit it, but part of me was curious about the challenge of making a sandwich while flying a rocket ship. That's the problem with deciding you're going to quit: things go and get *interesting* on you at the last minute.

I pulled out the first slice of bread. Laying it on the inside of the lid, I tried to get a second look at the how-to guide but found it impossible to read as the words shook, jumped, circled, and did everything but stand still. Fortunately I'd pretty much memorized the guidelines before boarding the ship.

SSSHHHOOOooooooooooo

The rocket tipped all the way up to a near vertical position, and the contents of the box nearly flew up into my face: I slapped a hand on top of them just in time. Then, using my elbow, I pushed down a lever that brought the ship level again.

"If you haven't sliced the meat yet you better hop to it!" said Chibb. "It only gets harder from here on out!"

I should just cry blue right now and get it over with, I thought. My hands weren't listening to me, though. They'd found the meat and the knife and were getting ready to make the first crucial eighth-inch slice.

"Space debris!" cried Chibb.

Space debris? What is that *supposed to mea—*

FWAM!

Something battered the ship on its left side. This was no simple sound effect: a big, heavy object was somehow rigged to slam into the rocket whenever Chibb desired. The knife slid from my fingers and clattered to the floor.

I knew he'd find a way to make me blow this.

FWA-FWAM!

A second object smacked the ship on the right side, more forcefully than the first. At the same time Chibb rotated the ship into a nosedive position and pumped up the vibration level by several notches.

Forget it. Cry blue already!

But my hands reached down to the floor and—to my surprise—recovered the knife. with very little fuss. Using my knees on one lever and my forehead on another, I managed to stabilize the ship without losing my grip on the sandwich.

FWAM, FWAM, FWA-FWAM!

I began to discern a certain pattern to the blows of the space debris, and was soon able to anticipate their arrival to a certain extent. I created a system for slicing the meat only when it was safe to do so. But just when I'd gotten to the last slice . . .

"Nitro-groxide leak!"

FFFSHHHHHHhhhhhhhhhh

Pale green gas began to spray into the cockpit from just behind my left shoulder. I coughed once, twice, then launched into a barrage of coughs that I knew wouldn't stop until the end of the exercise. Gasping for air, I grabbed hold of a dial with my teeth and switched on a ventilation system that blew most of the nitro-groxide out of the cockpit.

"I sure hope you're done with the condiments by now!" cried Chibb.

FWA-FWAM, FWA-FWAM!

My eyes were watering like crazy from the nitro-groxide. I stacked the slices of meat on the bottom piece of bread as neatly as I could and began applying the first of the three condiments: not too much, not too little.

"I'll show you, Chibb Fallaby," I whispered to myself between coughs. "I don't care how badly you want me to fail!" Suddenly there was no longer any question of my crying blue. I was going to complete this exercise no matter what.

I finished up with the condiments. A little messy—the gunk was all over my hands and shirt by then—but well within the guidelines. All I had to do was get the veggies on and I'd be done.

"Fire in the cockpit!"

Oh, you've got to be kidding me.

A burst of orange sparks suddenly erupted right in the middle of the dashboard. They sputtered and flew, pelting me in the face and arms. There was very little smoke—I think the designers knew that anything on top of the nitro-groxide would just knock you unconscious—but the heat was incredible. Within seconds the cockpit was like a furnace.

So that's *why there's so much sweat in here!*

It didn't matter, though: I had three of the four veggies squarely in place, and the fourth one on the way. I was coughing, and crying, and sweating a river down my face and my back, but there was no getting around it: I was excited.

This sandwich is perfect. I'm going to get an F, I just know it. An F!

Sparks stung my forehead and cheeks as I moved the final veggie into place (a furry green thing that looked like a week-old piece of roadkill) and reached for the second slice of bread. Pressing it down on top of the veggies, I shouted at the very top of my lungs: "Done! I'm done! I did it, *I did it!*"

Chibb switched off all the controls at once. The fire on the dashboard went out. The nitro-groxide stopped spraying. The rocket stopped humming and gently sank to the ground.

"Done, are you?" Chibb said as he popped the cockpit door open. "I'll be the judge of that."

I submitted the sandwich to his watchful eyes. He took it from my hands, held it in front of him, and carefully turned it around.

What would he say? Would he find some problem with it? Or would he finally admit that I'd done something well?

"This," he said, turning and showing it to Mr. Beeba and the others, "is really quite satisfactory, for a beginner." It was very faint praise, but there was no denying it. Chibb was impressed.

"Hoo-doggie!" cried Spuckler. "That is one ding-dang-*dandy* little sammich!"

I have no idea what I looked like at that moment, but I'm sure I was grinning like a fool. I was so proud I was ready to burst into tears.

Chibb looked me in the eye, the faintest trace of a smile on his lips.

"Not bad, child. Not bad at all."

My grade? Not first-rate, but distinguished: a D. The funny thing is suddenly I didn't even care about the grades anymore. All that mattered was that I'd gotten the job done.

Chapter 16

The rest of the afternoon sped by. Lessons were cut short at the end of the day because the training masters had to attend an official function—a ribbon-cutting ceremony or something like that—on a nearby planet. This meant that we were finally allowed a bit of rest and relaxation. Even though it was nothing more than an hour or two hanging around by our holes before dinner, it was like heaven to get a little free time after having had so little of it for the first couple of days.

The next morning in the Gathering Plaza we all stood waiting for our training masters as usual. For some reason, they were taking an awfully long time to arrive.

K'CHAK

All eyes turned to the door of the training masters' quarters. No training masters emerged, though. Instead, a short, plump alien in Zarga Baffa uniform waddled forward and delivered a brief message to all the trainees: "May I have your attention, please? I have some unpleasant news to share with you all this morning. As some of you may be aware, all the training masters left Zarga Baffa yesterday evening to attend a ribbon-cutting ceremony on the planet Yorbi. They were given the honor of being the first passengers aboard the new Virpling Canyon Cruiser."

There were envious murmurings among the trainees. The Canyon Cruiser was evidently something they'd all heard about.

"Due to a disastrous technical failure, the training masters are now trapped inside the cruiser, suspended high above Virpling Canyon."

The murmurs were replaced by horrified gasps.

The training masters were in trouble! It hardly seemed possible. I raised my hand and asked a question without waiting to be called on: "What's holding them above the canyon? A bridge or something?"

"No, no," said the little alien. "There is no bridge. The cruiser is attached to an enormous cable stretching from one side of Virpling Canyon to the other. Once the training masters have escaped from the inside of the cruiser, they will simply climb across the top of the cable to safety."

"But if it was that easy they would have escaped already," I whispered to Spuckler before raising my voice to ask another question. "Is there an escape hatch?"

"Yes, yes," said the alien, clearly flustered by my

questions. "They'll have it opened just as soon as they've discovered a way to do so without sending them plunging to the bottom of the . . . er . . ." The alien found himself in the middle of a sentence he didn't want to complete. He abandoned it and launched several new ones in its place: "Please don't worry. Everything's fine. The training masters are not in any danger of anything dangerous . . . er . . . endangering them."

A buzz went through the crowd of trainees, which the little alien hushed with frantic motions of his hands.

"Please remain calm. All is well, I assure you. The training masters will extricate themselves from the situation, but it could be some time before they are able to do so. In the meantime, I have been instructed to have you all return to your holes and wait for further orders."

The alien went back through the door. All the trainees immediately began the long trek back to the holes, everyone jabbering at once about the significance of this new development. I grabbed Mr. Beeba by the arm and motioned to the others that we should stay back and become the last in line.

"We can't just go back to our holes," I said. "We've got to rescue the training masters."

"RESCUE THEM?" said Gax. "BUT HOW?"

"Here's my plan. We find some sort of transportation, fly to the planet Yorbi, and go to this Virpling Canyon place. Then we can climb across the cable, use some of Gax's tools to open the Canyon Cruiser from the outside, and get the training masters out before their situation gets any worse than it already is."

"Now, now, Akiko," said Mr. Beeba, "it seems to me awfully presumptuous of you to be talking this way. Why, yesterday all you could talk about was crying blue and running back home."

"This is different," I said. "This isn't just another lesson. This is for real."

"Yes, but we were told to go back to our holes and await further orders. You can't just ignore rules and regulations whenever they don't suit you. I'm sure they've got a very efficient system in place for these sorts of—"

"Forget about the system." I turned to Spuckler, Gax, and Poog. "Think of the training masters. They're trapped inside that cruiser, and they could fall to the bottom of the canyon at any time. They need help. *Our* help. And if it means breaking the rules . . . hey, some rules *deserve* to be broken."

Spuckler nodded.

" 'Kiko's right. The trainin' masters must be in a mighty tough spot. They'd have got themselves out by now if they weren't."

Mr. Beeba said nothing, but I could see it in his eyes: Spuckler was right about this, and there was no denying it.

"Time's a-wastin'," said Spuckler. "Us loungin' around in our holes ain't gonna do nobody a lick of good."

I turned to Poog. "What do you say, Poog?"

Poog paused before answering. When he finally

spoke, his response was longer and more in-depth than I had expected. The warbly Toogolian syllables followed one another in rapid succession. Mr. Beeba's jaw dropped. He looked as if he didn't want to translate what he was hearing. When Poog finally stopped talking, there was a long silence.

"Well, c'mon, Beebs," said Spuckler. "Spit it out!"

"Poog says . . ." Mr. Beeba frowned and adjusted his spectacles. "Poog says the situation is far more dire than has been revealed. He senses that the training masters are in a very precarious state, that their lives are quite literally hanging by a thread."

"That does it," I said. "We've got to go, and we've got to go right now." I watched as the last of the trainees disappeared over a distant hill. "Now, listen. The other day when that nognag went haywire, I went straight through a hangar filled with spare astroshuttles. It's not that far from here, just a minute or two if we run. I say we borrow one of those astroshuttles and get to Virpling Canyon as fast as we can."

"Borrow?" said Mr. Beeba. "You mean *steal*! Flying off in one of Zarga Baffa's astroshuttles without permission . . . why, it could be grounds for expulsion!"

"I'm sure it is," I said. "But at least we'll know we tried to do the right thing, instead of sitting around here playing it safe. C'mon, Mr. Beeba. We're a team. We can't do this without you."

Mr. Beeba cast a mournful glance back at the doorway to the training masters' quarters.

"I'm going to regret this," he said.

Chapter 17

Within minutes we were making our way through the Zarga Baffa complex toward the astroshuttle hangar, moving on our hands and knees so that no one would see us.

"That's the sports field over there," I said as I took a quick peek over a wall. "So the hangar should be . . . *Bingo!*" There it was, one of its big sliding doors wide open.

"The hangar should be bingo?" asked Spuckler.

"Bingo," I said. "It's an expression."

"What's it mean?"

"What does *bingo* mean?" I scratched the side of my head. "Well, it means, um . . . I don't really know, actually. It's just a word. Sort of like *voilà*."

"Vwah-Lah?" said Mr. Beeba. "As in the Vwah-Lah galaxy?"

"There's a galaxy named Vwah-Lah?" I asked. "No way."

"And there's a planet called Bingo, come to think of it," said Mr. Beeba. "But the stress is on the second syllable rather than the fir—"

"I HATE TO INTERRUPT THIS SCINTILLATING CONVERSATION," said Gax, "BUT SOMEONE IS CLOSING THE DOOR TO THE HANGAR."

Sure enough, a big hairy security guard in a Zarga Baffa uniform was pulling the door shut.

"You guys go ahead," said Spuckler as he jumped to his feet. "I'll distract him."

"But Spuckler!" I said. Too late: he was already gone, off to do whatever it was he planned on doing.

"Don't worry, Akiko," said Mr. Beeba. "I'm sure he won't do anything crazy."

I gave Mr. Beeba a sideways glance.

Mr. Beeba furrowed his brow, reconsidering what he'd just said. "Well, no crazier than usual, anyway."

Suddenly, from Spuckler's direction: "*YOOOOoooo-HOOOOoooooooo!*"

The hairy guy stopped shutting the door and turned his head to see what was going on.

"Over here, fuzzy face!" Spuckler was standing up on a wall a good fifty yards away from the hangar door, shaking his butt from side to side and flinging his hands around in ways that can only be described as moves from the golden age of disco. "Wanna dance?"

The security guard growled and took several big stomps in Spuckler's direction. He barked something in an alien language that needed no translating. This guy did *not* want to dance.

You are a madman, Spuckler, I thought. I turned my eyes to the still-open door. There was just enough space for all of us to squeeze through. *And a madman is just what we need right now.*

"Come on, guys," I said. "This is the only chance we're going to get."

Mr. Beeba, Gax, Poog, and I all dashed to the hangar door and slipped inside. Poking my head back out, I saw Spuckler running circles around the furious security guard, who was throwing wild punches at him and missing every time.

"Dang, that's some mighty fine hoofin' there!" cackled Spuckler. "You been takin' lessons?"

I didn't want to blow our cover, but time was running out.

"Spuckler!" I whispered as loudly as I dared. "Get over here!"

The security guard spun to face me. His face twisted into an angry scowl as he understood the trick that had been played on him.

"Thanks for the dance, pardner!" said Spuckler. He dashed to the door and leaped through, seconds before Mr. Beeba and I closed and locked it. What followed was the sound of one very angry security guard: two furious fists pounding like thunder and a barrage of shouted threats I was glad I didn't understand.

"Spuckler, you idiot!" said Mr. Beeba. "Now all of Zarga Baffa will know what we're up to!"

"Which is why we gotta vamoose," said Spuckler as he trotted over to the first available astroshuttle, "and I mean right now, pronto!"

We didn't have the luxury of questioning Spuckler. The guard would get in through another entrance soon enough, and this time he probably wouldn't be alone.

Spuckler jumped into the driver's seat and revved the engine. "Virpling Canyon," he said as Mr. Beeba, Gax, Poog, and I piled into the back of the ship, "here we come!"

There was no exit big enough for the astroshuttle except for the one we'd just locked, so Spuckler did the next best thing. He blasted us out through one of the windows. This brought the number of Zarga Baffa rules we'd broken to a grand total of nine (as Mr. Beeba angrily pointed out, listing them all in great detail), and somewhere deep down I wondered if it was really okay to be doing all this stuff: sneaking around, tricking security guards, borrowing astroshuttles.

It's all in the name of rescuing the training masters, I told myself. *That makes it okay.*

I looked out the windows of the astroshuttle as we rocketed into the morning sky, leaving Zarga Baffa behind.

Or pretty close to okay, anyway.

Chapter 18

It didn't take us very long to get to the planet Yorbi. As we zoomed down to its surface, the astroshuttle began to rock from side to side and make sudden, unpredictable movements.

"Zallamite," said Spuckler. "There ain't nothin' a rocket pilot hates worse."

"Zallamite?" I asked.

"A fascinating type of mineral, Akiko," said Mr. Beeba. "Virpling Canyon is practically built of the stuff. As it happens, I wrote an exhaustive essay on Zallamite back in graduate school." His eyes glazed over as he recalled what must have been one of his greatest achievements. "Ah, yes, and what an essay it was! The bibliography alone was no less than forty-eight pages long. My professor said it was one of the best geological treatises he'd ever seen. Or the heaviest, at any rate. Why, I even submitted it to the *Intergalactic Journal of Geolo*—"

"Cut to the chase, Beebs!" said Spuckler. "You're gonna put the girl to sleep!"

Mr. Beeba shot Spuckler an irritated glance.

"*Ahem.* The long and short of it is that Zallamite emits ultrasonic waves that interfere with the antigravity cells of rocket ships. That's why the people of Yorbi had to attach the Canyon Cruiser to a cable in the first place. There's no way of getting anywhere near the canyon with a conventional flying vehicle."

Gax, who had a complete map of the planet Yorbi programmed into him, served as our navigator. "IF WE MAKE OUR APPROACH FROM THE SOUTH, WE WILL BE ABLE TO GET RELATIVELY CLOSE TO THE CANYON BEFORE HAVING TO COMPLETE THE JOURNEY ON FOOT." He paused, examining his own robot body, and added: "OR ON *WHEEL,* AS THE CASE MAY BE."

"Thank ya, Gax," said Spuckler, struggling to maintain his control over the ship. "I hope everybody's got them seat belts buckled, 'cause I reckon we're in for a pretty rough landing."

The closer we got to Virpling Canyon, the wilder the astroshuttle's movements became. Spuckler wasn't pressing the brakes, though. On the contrary, he shifted the astroshuttle into its highest gear and gunned the accelerator.

"Spuckler, you maniac!" cried Mr. Beeba as the ship nearly smashed into a huge outcropping of stone. "You're supposed to be slowing down, not speeding up!"

"No can do, Beebs," said Spuckler. "I got a plan."

"A plan!" Mr. Beeba shrieked as the ship glanced off a wall of stone and whizzed through a narrow ravine. "Your so-called plan is going to kill us all!"

"Nope," said Spuckler. "It's gonna *nearly* kill us all. That's the sign of a real good plan!"

Soon the ship began swerving and lurching so violently it was impossible to see what was going on. I shut my eyes, held on to my seat, and braced myself for a crash.

FLOOOOOOOooooooooom

Spuckler killed the engine the moment the bottom of the astroshuttle began to skid across the ground. The windows turned yellow orange as we tunneled through a big, thick dust cloud of our own making. The ceiling rattled and the walls groaned. We kept skidding until we slowed to a crawl and gradually came to a complete stop.

All at once the ship became dead quiet. There wasn't a sound apart from the winds of Yorbi whistling by outside as the dust began to clear.

"Welcome to Virpling Canyon," said Spuckler, turning and tipping an imaginary bus driver's cap. "Please watch yer step as you exit the vehicle."

Mr. Beeba's grumbling turned to a gasp as we jumped out and saw that Spuckler had somehow managed to make the astroshuttle skid all the way to the very edge of Virpling Canyon. The nose of the ship was even poking *over* the edge a little. If we'd gone even a few feet farther, we'd have all plunged to our deaths.

"Wow, Spuckler," I said. "You weren't kidding when you said you might *nearly* kill us all."

"Actually, I was," Spuckler said as he peered down into the canyon. "I was figurin' we'd come to a stop way back there," he added, pointing to a spot about a hundred yards behind us. "But hey, no harm done, right?"

Mr. Beeba shuddered and said nothing, evidently having run out of variations on the word *lunatic*.

"All right," I said, "we're here. Now we've got to get to the Canyon Cruiser as quickly as we can. Who knows how much time the training masters have left."

Gax led the way around the edge of the cliffs to the Canyon Cruiser boarding station. The winds increased the farther we went, and by the time the station came into view it felt like we were making our way through a small tornado.

Finally we reached the entrance to the building, which served as a very welcome shelter from the storm. Inside there were several rows of benches, a ticket office, and a concession stand, all empty. On one side of the room, before a window overlooking the canyon, was a group of about a dozen men with green skin and big yellow eyes: the Yorbians who were in charge of the Canyon Cruiser. They were surrounded by reporters, most of whom were taking photographs and asking a barrage of questions. When the Yorbians saw us, they pointed excitedly.

"They're here! They're here!"

The reporters immediately swarmed to our side, snapping at us with their strange alien cameras.

One of the Yorbians cut through the crowd to greet us. "Thank goodness you're here! Which one of you is the leader?" he said. Spuckler and Mr. Beeba pointed at me and the Yorbian shook my hand vigorously. "It's a miracle that you made the trip from the planet Wezzlo so quickly! I really don't know how you did it."

The planet Wezzlo?

Before I could say anything in response, the Yorbian turned to the reporters and spoke loudly and triumphantly. "Ladies and gentlemen, the situation is now very much under control. This is the crew of space patrollers we have called in to bring the passengers back to safety. I have every confidence in them. They are from the planet Wezzlo, and have glorious record of successful rescue missions under their belts."

The reporters shouted questions and there was an explosion of flashbulbs.

I shot a glance at Spuckler and Mr. Beeba. It was clearly a case of mistaken identity, but under the circumstances explaining who we really were seemed like a waste of precious time. I turned to the Yorbian and put on my best professional face.

"So, uh, if you can brief us on the situation, we'll get to work right away."

"But of course, of course."

The Yorbian led us through the crowd to the window. Through it we could see a gigantic cable stretching from one side of the canyon to the other, and, hundreds of yards away, the Canyon Cruiser itself. It was like one of those cable cars you see sometimes at ski resorts, the kind that carries sight-seers straight up to the top of a mountain.

"It's this sudden sandstorm that's created this mess," said the Yorbian. "It came from out of nowhere just as the Canyon Cruiser's maiden voyage began. You can see the damage it's caused already."

I could see it, all right. The cruiser was supposed to be attached to the cable in three places. One of its connectors had broken, and a second was severely damaged. The whole ship was now swaying perilously from side to side, and in danger of plummeting to the bottom of the canyon.

"No wonder they're having problems getting out of that thing," I said. "Every move they make could snap that second connector."

"Quite right," said the Yorbian. "To make matters worse, a twisted girder is blocking the escape hatch in the roof. There's really no way for them to get out on their own."

"All right, come on," I said to the Yorbian. "You've got to get us up to the cable so we can climb across it."

"Right this way," said the Yorbian, leading us up a stairwell to the roof.

"But Akiko," said Mr. Beeba as we made our way up the steps, "in these winds we'll never be able to hold on to that cable. We'll get blown off into the canyon before we get even halfway across."

"There's a chance of that happening," I said. "I won't deny it. But it's a risk we're going to have to take if we're going to rescue the training masters."

When we got to the roof of the building, the wind was stronger than ever. Sand stung my face, and I had to lean to one side just to keep from being blown over. The wind made a loud and eerie noise, like the yowling of a pack of wolves.

"There!" shouted the Yorbian, pointing at a huge tower from which the cable was suspended. "That's the way up to the cable."

Getting to the cable looked simple enough; there was a ladder leading straight up to it. But Mr. Beeba was right about the wind. It would make crawling across the top of the cable almost impossible.

"Don't worry," I said to the Yorbian as we left him behind us. "We've got everything under control."

"Thank you!" he yelled before going back to deal with the reporters. "We will put up a very nice monument in your honor if by chance you all get killed."

I wished he hadn't said that.

One by one we climbed the tower and made our way to the cable. It was about four feet across, the size of a good strong tree trunk. Its surface was pretty smooth, though, and would be very hard to get a good grip on. Spuckler went first, followed by Gax, then me, then Poog and Mr. Beeba. I watched as Spuckler crawled out across the cable and Gax inched his way after him. Poog was lucky: he simply used his powers of levitation to float wherever he pleased. The rest of us had to just hold on as best we could.

Don't look down, I told myself as I reached the point where the cable passed over the canyon. *Just stay focused on the Canyon Cruiser.*

The wind whipped my jeans and jacket back and forth like a flag on a flagpole. It howled so loudly in my ears I thought I might go deaf. The cable creaked and groaned as it swayed from side to side. Once I nearly lost my grip and slid off altogether. Only by tensing every muscle in my fingers, arms, and legs was I able to regain my balance and stay where I was.

I tried to gauge the distance between the Canyon Cruiser and us: about two hundred yards. Maybe more.

Though I didn't let myself look down, I knew the stomach-churning truth about how high I was above the bottom of the canyon. You could have built a skyscraper in the canyon with room to spare.

Spuckler came to a stop and called back to the rest of us. All I caught was the word *news,* which I really hoped wasn't the second half of the phrase *bad news.*

It was.

As I neared Spuckler, it became clear just how bad the news was. From this point onward the cable was covered with a thin film of grease, making it even harder to keep a good grip. For Gax, sadly, it meant going no farther. The grease would have made his suction cups almost useless.

"You hold the fort here, little buddy," said Spuckler. "We'll be right back."

"I'M SORRY, SIR," said Gax, a sad squeak in his mechanical voice. "I'VE LET YOU DOWN."

"Aw, now, you know that ain't true, Gax. We're gonna needja when we get those fellas out of the cruiser. Just stay put. Your time'll come!"

I told Spuckler to remove a couple of things from inside Gax: a long piece of rope and his welder's torch. I knew we'd need both of them.

Mr. Beeba and I crawled around Gax, both of us offering him words of encouragement as we passed. Poog took Gax's place behind Spuckler, and on we went.

By now we were nearly halfway out to the Canyon Cruiser. The wind howled and roared, chilling me to the bone.

We've got to keep going. The training masters' lives depend on it.

No matter how awful or scary it became, I kept stretching one hand in front of the other, pulling myself forward inch by inch.

"Most air!" I heard Spuckler cry, though I'm pretty sure what he'd really said was "We're almost there!"

I looked up. Sure enough, the Canyon Cruiser was no more than sixty or seventy feet away. If we could all just keep from . . .

FFFWWWWWOOOOOOoooooosssssshhhh!

All at once a gust of wind blasted me so hard I felt my legs rising into the air. I tried to dig my hands into the threaded surface of the cable, but it was no use: my fingers slipped, slid, then lost their grip altogether.

"Heeeeeeeeeellllp!"

At the last possible moment I felt a hand clamp around my ankle, hold me in space, and then gradually pull me back to safety. For a good thirty seconds all I could do was hold on to the cable for dear life, hugging it as if it were the best friend I'd ever had. Then I turned my head and saw Mr. Beeba behind me, one yellow-gloved hand still locked around my ankle.

"Really now, little lady!" he shouted before flashing me a grin. "Stunts like *that* we could do without!"

How do you thank someone for saving your life? Well, if you're me, you end up coughing, wheezing, and saying something like this: "Thank you, Mr. Beeba! Thank you!" I meant it. Meant it with all my heart. "That . . . that was close!"

"I'll say!" Mr. Beeba let go of my ankle and motioned me onward. "Now keep moving! We've got some catching up to do!"

Chapter 19

Finally we got to the place where the Canyon Cruiser was connected to the cable. Spuckler turned to me and put one hand on my shoulder.

"The cruiser can't handle much more weight than she's already got! Me and Beeba . . . we're too heavy. It's gonna have to be you and Poog."

"Right," I said. "That's where this stuff comes in." I took Gax's torch and stuck it in my pocket. Then I took the rope and tied one end of it around my chest, just below my armpits. "This will serve as my safety net in case I fall." I gave the other end to Spuckler.

"Gotcha!"

I swallowed hard and looked down at the roof of

the Canyon Cruiser, swaying endlessly back and forth in the wind. The Yorbian was right: there was a good-sized emergency hatch at one end, but when the car had come loose from its riggings, a girder had smashed down on top of the door, barring the passengers' only means of escape. If we were really lucky, it would be a simple matter of bending that girder out of the way.

"All right," I said. "Let's go, Poog."

The wind blasted me as I crawled down the second connector to the roof of the Canyon Cruiser. Even from a distance I'd been able to see that this connector was weak, but a closer inspection revealed just how threadbare it really was. Only three wrist-thick pieces of steel kept it from snapping in half, and all three of them were badly twisted and stretched out of shape.

Maybe they're stronger than they look, I thought. *Man, I sure hope they are.*

I continued making my way down, one careful

inch at a time. Compared to groping my way across the grease-covered cable, climbing down the connector was pretty easy. There were wires and pieces of steel to hold on to, and the rope tied around me offered about as much security as I could have hoped for. Plus I had Poog at my side the whole time. With his encouraging smile nearby, I knew I'd have help when I needed it.

There was a complicating factor, though: the noises.

GREEEEeeeeeeeee
ROOOOOooooooooooo
The cruiser produced the most horrible squeaks and screeches imaginable. Eerie

groans filled the air with every pendulum swing it made, sending chills down the back of my neck and making my flesh crawl. Add the nonstop howl of the wind and you've got one surefire case of the heebie-jeebies.

When I reached the bottom of the connector, I put one foot down on the roof, then the other, shifting my weight as slowly as I could. The Canyon Cruiser let off a whole new batch of squeals and moans but seemed capable of supporting me for the time being.

"All right, Poog," I said. "Let's have a look at this escape hatch."

The hatch was easy to lift, but the girder bent across it prevented me from opening it any more than a crack. I placed my mouth as close to the gap as I could and shouted down into the Canyon Cruiser, "Is everyone okay down there?"

There was a commotion below as the training masters realized their rescue might finally be at hand.

"Who is that?" said a voice that I recognized as that of Odo Mumzibar.

"Akiko," I said, "from the planet Earth. I'm here to get you all out of this thing."

There was a storm of questions and answers among the training masters.

"Be careful, Akiko," said Odo. "You're putting yourself in a very dangerous position here."

"I'll be as careful as I can, sir," I said.

"And good luck, dear child," Odo added. "We'll all be needing it!"

I gave Poog a smile. "Luck?" I whispered. "What we need is a miracle."

I placed both my hands on the girder and pulled as hard as I could. It was no use. This thing was solid steel, nearly a foot wide. After several exhausting minutes of pushing, pulling, tugging, and heaving with all my might, I had to just give up.

Okay. Time for plan B.

I knocked on the roof of the Canyon Cruiser with my fists, searching for a hollow spot. I found one just a few feet from the base of the second connector. Then I pulled Gax's torch out of my pocket, held it away from myself, and pushed a button on its side.

FRAAAAW!

A powerful blast of fire shot out of its tip, warming my face and bathing Poog and me in yellow-orange light. I lowered the flame to the roof of the Canyon Cruiser and began tracing a burning line into the metal.

FFFSSSSSSHHHHhhhhhhhhh

Sparks flew everywhere as the torch melted its way through the steel. My fingers were burning from the heat, but that was something I'd just have to live with: they'd be burning a whole lot more by the time I was done.

I moved the torch in a clockwise direction, slowly cutting a large circle in the roof. I figured if I could get even three-quarters of the way around, I'd be able to kick it in and have a brand-new exit to work with.

Soon I had the job nearly halfway done. My fingers were red from the sparks and flames, but if I could take the pain just a little bit longer . . .

Suddenly Poog cried out. I turned and found him examining the second connector. It was twisting, turning, growing weaker and weaker. If it snapped, only one connector would remain. Then the whole Canyon Cruiser would swing down to a vertical position. Who knew, it might even fall off the cable altogether.

GREEEEeeeeeeeeee

ROOOOOooooooooooo

The three remaining bars of the second connector began to splinter and crack. Then . . .

BAM!

   BAM!

      BAAAAM!

. . . it exploded into fragments. My stomach leaped into my throat as the roof of the Canyon Cruiser dropped out from underneath me. The rope—the only thing keeping me from plunging to the bottom of Virpling Canyon—dug in under my armpits and cut into my skin.

Everything around me blurred. It took several seconds to regain my bearings. I crammed Gax's torch back into my pocket and reached up to grab the rope with both hands. I feared the worst, that the Canyon Cruiser had broken free from the cable altogether and was already gone.

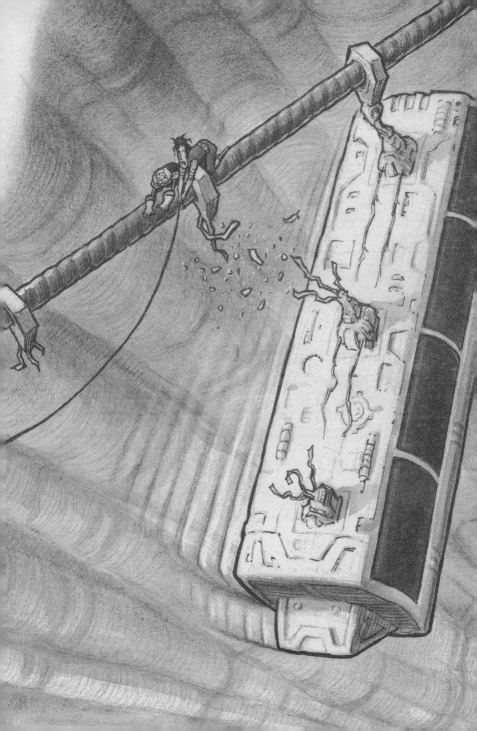

Chapter 20

Talk about miracles: the first connector was still in place. There was the Canyon Cruiser, no more than ten yards away from me. It was pitched at the extreme angle of a sinking ship, swinging from side to side, creaking and groaning more loudly than ever.

" 'Kiko!" I heard Spuckler cry from above. "Hold on! I'm gonna pull ya back up!"

For an instant my eyes looked downward at the horrifying chasm just beyond the tips of my tennis shoes, the pale orange ground many thousands of feet below me. *Yes,* I thought. *Pull me back up and get me out of here!*

But I couldn't forget the Canyon Cruiser. The

training masters were still trapped inside. It could be just a matter of seconds before the last connector gave way and . . .

"No!" I cried back to him. "We can't give up! It's not too late!"

"But 'Kiko—"

"Just swing me over to the cruiser! You can pull me up once we've rescued the training masters!"

Spuckler gave me a doubtful look but did as I asked. By swinging the rope back and forth, he got me to within a yard or two of the cruiser. By the third try, I was able to grab hold of a girder.

GREEEEeeeeeeeee

ROOOOOooooooooooo

Things were bad and getting worse. The one remaining connector was already severely twisted and was weakening with every move the Canyon Cruiser made.

I groped my way back to the half-finished hole in the roof, reached into my pocket, and fired up Gax's torch. Plunging it toward the spot where I'd left off,

I completed the circle and carefully pushed it inside. There was a loud clank as it landed somewhere on the interior of the Canyon Cruiser. I stuck my head through. There, huddled against the far end of the car, were all twenty-one of the training masters. Chibb Fallaby stared at me with his mouth open wide.

"She . . . ," he said, ". . . she didn't give up."

"Of *course* she didn't give up," said Odo Mumzibar with a grin. "She's no quitter."

"Well, come on!" I said. "Don't tell me you want to stay in here!"

They definitely didn't. Crawling up the floor of the cruiser, the training masters thanked me again and again. "It's okay, it's okay," I said. "The important thing right now is for all of us to get out of here."

I grabbed the hand of one of the training masters (a three-fingered hand with big lumps on the knuckles) and pulled him halfway through the hole. "Don't worry about hurting me. Just get on my shoulders and climb up the rope." He did as I asked. Two more of them got out the same way. I glanced up and watched as the first one climbed onto the top of the cable and received an enthusiastic greeting from Mr. Beeba. *All right,* I thought. *One down, twenty to go.*

Slowly but surely all the training masters climbed out of the Canyon Cruiser and made their way up the rope. Before long, I was helping the second to last—a wrinkled old guy with a long white beard—out of the hole. Only one training master remained: Chibb Fallaby.

GREEEEeeeeeeeee

ROOOOOooooooooo

A shudder ran through the cruiser. The last connector was beginning to fail.

GREEEEeeeeeeeee

ROOOOOooooooooo

Time was running out. I grabbed the old training master by the waist and pulled him out. "Quickly!" I shouted. *"Quickly!"*

The old man scampered onto my shoulders, then

pulled himself up the rope. As he did, an earsplitting screech erupted from the last connector.

KREEEEEEEEEeeeeeeeeeeeeeeeeeee

It was about to snap. There was no doubt about it.

"Come on!" I said to Chibb, who was still making his way up to me. As he put his hand in mine, a sudden gust of wind tossed the Canyon Cruiser into the air. I lost my grip and Chibb tumbled to the bottom of the car.

"Beeba!" I heard Spuckler cry. "Hold this!" He was trying to get Mr. Beeba to take over the rope-holding duties, which at this moment meant carrying the second-to-last training master as well as me. Would Mr. Beeba be able to support the weight?

"But Spuckler—"

"No buts!" Spuckler grabbed one of Mr. Beeba's hands and clamped it around the rope. "C'mon, fellas!" he hollered to the other training masters as he crawled across the cable to the top of the last connector. "We gotta shore this thing up before she blows!"

Spuckler and all the able-bodied training masters

climbed down the connector and turned themselves into living support beams, one hand clutching a girder above, one grasping a support beam on the roof of the Canyon Cruiser. It was nothing more than a stopgap measure, something to buy Chibb and me another few seconds.

"All right, Chibb!" I shouted. "It's now or never!"

There, shaking and whimpering at the bottom of the car, was Chibb Fallaby. He had knocked himself in the head during his fall and was now in a daze. There was a glassy look in his eyes, and he had pulled his knees all the way up to his chest. "I'll never be a real training master," he was saying to himself over and over.

A real training master? Chibb's not a real training master?

It didn't matter.

"Chibb, you've got to move!" I cried. "I can get you out of this thing if you'll just climb up here!"

No response. He was totally out of it. It was as if he hadn't heard a word I'd said.

KREEEEEEEEEEEeeeeeeeeeeeeeeeeeee

The connector was twisting, turning, pulling Spuckler and the training masters back and forth as it began to give way altogether.

"Chibb!" I shouted at the top of my lungs. "Don't flimp on me! Get off the floor and climb up here! *Now!*" For an instant I was thrust into the role of training master, urging this quivering young man to pull himself together and give his all. "I . . . said . . . *now!*"

This seemed to snap Chibb out of his stupor. He looked around for a moment, recognizing where he was and what was at stake. A look of strength and determination returned to his face, and—with surprising speed and agility—he climbed the steep slope of the Canyon Cruiser floor and thrust his hand into mine.

BAM!

BAM!

BAAAAM!

The last connector splintered into fragments. There was nothing holding the Canyon Cruiser up but the tensed muscles of Spuckler and the training masters. Poog shot down and positioned himself beneath the far end of the cruiser, providing a crucial last bit of support.

Chibb leaped out onto my shoulder as . . .

"Nnnnnnggggh!"

"Aaaaarrrrrggggghh!"

. . . Spuckler and the training masters all lost their grip. The Canyon Cruiser tipped back off Poog and tumbled, end over end . . .

. . . end over end . . .

. . . end over end . . .

. . . straight to the bottom of Virpling Canyon.

I watched with a strange feeling of satisfaction as it struck the ground and vanished in a cloud of orange dust.

Chapter 21

We all made our way across the top of the cable and back to the boarding station. We were nearly smothered by the reporters and photographers congratulating us and asking questions in about a dozen different languages. Mr. Beeba spoke on behalf of all of us, telling them that for the moment the most important thing was to get back to Zarga Baffa and make sure all the training masters were in good health. The Yorbians thanked us again and again, promising gifts and statues in our honor.

We returned to Zarga Baffa. When we arrived, there was a big crowd waiting for us: trainees, training camp employees, and a small group of doctors ready to examine the training masters. Everyone cheered as we emerged from the ship. Well, everyone but Dregger and his crew, who would have been green with envy except that they were all green to begin with.

Spuckler, Gax, Mr. Beeba, Poog, and I were allowed to wash up and rest awhile in the Zarga Baffa bathhouse. It was the first warm water I'd touched in days, and soaking in it was pure heaven. I'd have stayed there all day if they had let me.

A few hours later, though, we were all escorted to a part of the Zarga Baffa complex we'd never seen before: a large, brightly lit space with a big, long table, a couple dozen chairs, and hardly anything else. After a minute or two we were joined by Odo Mumzibar and six of the most senior training masters. Chibb Fallaby was not among them.

"Good afternoon," said Odo Mumzibar. "First of all, I want to offer all of you our deepest gratitude for the stupendous efforts you made this morning. Truly it was one of the greatest rescue missions I have ever been party to, and, it must be said, the only one in which I have been among those being rescued. We owe the five of you a debt that can never be properly repaid."

"Ya could start with some good food, though," Spuckler said, and I kicked him hard in the leg.

"Nevertheless," Odo Mumzibar continued, "you have put us in a rather difficult position. A number of your activities this morning were entirely illegal, even if we apply the very loosest interpretation of Zarga Baffa rules. Stealing rocket ships, leaving the training camp without permission . . ." He paused and raised an eyebrow at Spuckler. ". . . dancing with security guards." Spuckler turned a deep shade of red. "As grateful as I am to you for having rescued all of us, I am compelled to point out your disregard for Zarga Baffa procedure. I am torn between congratulating you on a job well done and punishing you for the reckless way in which you did it."

He paused for a very long time, staring each of us in the eye for a good second or two. "However, there are certain aspects of this case that bear consideration."

He leaned forward in his chair, staring deeply into the surface of the table.

"First there is the matter of Chibb Fallaby. As you are probably now aware, he is not a true training master. Not yet." He kept his eyes on the table for a moment, as if he hoped to find the words he wanted to say written somewhere upon it.

"Full training master status was to be conferred upon him within the year. When the Smoovian king asked that you and your friends be included in this year's class of trainees, we were caught short. Rather than send you away, we granted Fallaby honorary training master status for the duration of your lessons." He paused for a deep sigh, then continued. "One could argue that his inexperience played a part in your willingness to dispense with Zarga Baffa rules."

He raised his eyes to mine for a moment, shook his head ever so slightly, then spoke. "There is one further matter." He turned and called to someone waiting outside the doorway. "Miss Kayooli, you may enter now."

Raspa entered the room. She wore an angry

frown and shuffled across the floor in long, slow steps that suggested she would rather be somewhere else. Anywhere else.

Odo Mumzibar regarded Raspa for a moment, then waved his hand at her, as if she were an actress who had forgotten her lines. "Your apology."

"I . . ." Her eyes moved around the room, carefully avoiding mine. "I'm sorry, Akiko."

"Go on," said Odo. "Tell her what you did."

"I lied to you about Chibb Fallaby." Raspa's eyes went to the ceiling. "It wasn't Chibb's brother who got sick on the planet Earth. It was *my* brother. I'm the one who hates Earthians, not Chibb. I was trying to trick you into crying blue."

I shot a startled glance at Odo Mumzibar, who nodded, assuring me that it was all true.

"There's more," he said to me, then turned to Raspa. "Isn't there?"

"Yes." There was a quaver in her voice. I could tell she really didn't want to go on but was forcing herself to spit the words out. "I fired a dart into the nognag you were riding the other day. That was . . . that was what made it go crazy." Raspa closed her mouth. I think she'd reached the limits of what she could say without bursting into tears.

Odo Mumzibar tossed a clear plastic bag onto the table. It contained Raspa's little red dart gun. "Raspa is a very able student. It's a shame she wasted her abilities on such a petty scheme." He raised his eyes to meet mine. "Do you have anything to say to her, Akiko?"

I looked at Raspa. I actually felt a little sorry for her. She had suffered a lot because of what had happened to her brother. She didn't need me adding to her pain.

"Yes," I said. "I accept your apology, Raspa, and I hope that you won't be expelled because of what you did."

"You are generous, Akiko," said Odo. "We will take your thoughts into consideration when it comes time to decide Raspa's fate." He nodded at Raspa, who bowed and left the room. Once she was gone, Odo turned to face me one last time.

"As for you and your friends," Odo said, "it is the opinion of this council that the rules you broke this morning are more than compensated for by the valor and selflessness with which you performed the mission. There will be no punishment for the rules broken, and you will be allowed to continue your training." He gave us all a very severe look and raised a finger. "If you can refrain from breaking any more Zarga Baffa rules, I see no reason why you all shouldn't graduate within the normal allotted time." He paused, then asked, "Any questions?"

"Yes," I said. "Will Chibb Fallaby still be our training master?"

Odo smiled at my question. "Do you *want* him to be your training master?"

I looked around and saw that all eyes were on

me. Were they putting me in charge of such a big decision? Definitely not. I was simply being asked my opinion. One thing's for sure, though: everyone was very curious to hear what I would say.

"Yes," I said. "I do." I was still angry at Chibb about a few things. A *lot* of things, actually. But I wanted to finish what I'd started with him, one way or another.

"Interesting," said Odo. "Go to the Gathering Plaza. Your training master is waiting for you there." He then brought the meeting to a close.

When we got to the Gathering Plaza, there was Chibb, smiling and brimming with confidence. He explained that Odo Mumzibar had decided to delay his transition to full master status, but only by a few months.

As for our rescue mission at Virpling Canyon, Chibb only spoke of it once, then never brought the subject up again: "Thanks for saving me, Akiko. I'd be a dead man right now if not for you."

"You're welcome, Chibb." I grinned. "I wasn't going to let you get out of being my training master *that* easily."

Chibb laughed, then adopted a mock-serious tone to do his best impersonation of me: *"Don't flimp on me! Get off the ground and climb up here!"* He gave me a wink. "Better watch yourself, Akiko. You'll end up being a mean old training master like me."

Chapter 22

The rest of our stay on Zarga Baffa went pretty smoothly. I'm not saying it was easy. Far from it. The second half of Humbling Week was, if anything, even worse than the first half. But by that time I'd developed a pretty thick skin. If I had a bad lesson, I had a bad lesson. It was no biggie; I just moved on to the next one and tried to do better. And I *did* do better. By the end of the second week I was getting mostly D's and F's.

The third week was when we became advanced trainees, which meant we could finally sleep in real beds, eat delicious food, and get as much rest and relaxation as we needed. It was as wonderful as I'd imagined it would be, and then some. The lessons also changed. They were no longer about testing our endurance but about learning useful skills: laser beam target practice, alien first aid, how to recognize mutant Gorglezogs disguised as innocent bystanders. I was pretty good in all my classes, but I was especially good in a class called Intergalactic Conflict Resolution. Spuckler and Mr. Beeba had given me a lot of practice in that department.

On our last night there was a big dinner for all the graduating trainees, and everyone in the whole Zarga Baffa complex was there, even Grunn Grung, who sat in a shadowy corner of the room, sipping sludge from a bucket. Spuckler, Gax, Poog, Mr. Beeba, Chibb, and I all sat at one table. At one point the Yorbians showed up. They kept coming to our table and thanking us. One of them gave me a gift: a small jar full of orange goo. (They said rubbing it on my belly would fortify my microintestine. I told them I was pretty sure I didn't *have* a microintestine, but they didn't believe me.)

After the dinner was a brief graduation ceremony. We were all given diplomas certifying us as official Zarga Baffa space patrollers and declaring that we were fit to take part in any and all adventures throughout the universe. If those adventures involved having to make muzzlegup sandwiches while piloting rocket ships, so much the better. I wish King Froptoppit could have been there. I wanted to see the expression on his face when he learned that the planet Smoo finally had its own crew of certified space patrollers.

The next morning we joined the training masters and all the other trainees back at the platform where we had first arrived. A shiny new astroshuttle was waiting there to take us back home.

Before I boarded, Chibb Fallaby took me aside and shook my hand.

"Good luck on all your future adventures, Akiko," he said. "I know you'll make all of us here at Zarga Baffa very proud."

"Thanks, Chibb. And good luck to you on

becoming an official training master." I didn't want to admit it, but I'd learned a lot from him. He'd pushed me so hard I ended up seeing parts of myself I'd never seen before. Good stuff. Ugly stuff. The whole shebang. "You're . . ." I wanted to say something nice to him, but after everything he'd put me through, it was pretty much impossible. "You're a really tough teacher."

He smiled. "Oh yeah? Well, you, my friend, are one hardheaded, stubborn little cuss of a student."

I had to laugh. "You bet I am."

The flight back to Earth was a lot of fun. We chatted with all the other passengers about what we'd do when we got back home, what sorts of food we missed having while we were away, and all the adventures we hoped to have in the future.

When we got to the roof of the Fowlerville mall, there was the Akiko robot waiting for me. It was exactly three weeks later, and this time she was at the mall with my best friend, Melissa.

"You'd better hurry," the robot said to me as I jumped out of the astroshuttle and we switched places. "I told Melissa I was going to the bathroom. That was about half an hour ago."

"You've got to come up with a better plan next time. What am I going to tell her?"

"Don't worry," she said with a wink. "You're

getting really good at this. I'm sure you'll come up with something."

"See ya, 'Kiko," said Spuckler. "Don't go on any adventures without givin' us a holler first."

"What," I said, "and miss seeing who you choose for your next dancing partner? Not a chance."

The astroshuttle driver barked something at us. We'd have to cut our goodbyes short.

"Do take care, my dear," said Mr. Beeba. "We'll come back to see you again at the first opportunity."

"Great," I said. "And, hey, tell King Froptoppit I said thanks for everything. It was the best three weeks of my life, and the worst three weeks too."

"I know exactly what you mean," said Mr. Beeba before the doors slid shut. Poog smiled at me through the window as the astroshuttle rose into the air, and Gax waved goodbye with a spindly mechanical arm.

A moment later they rocketed into the sky and disappeared behind a bank of clouds. And that was the last time I saw them.

Well, for a while, anyway. I knew they'd be back for another adventure soon enough. But at that moment I wanted nothing more adventurous than an ordinary Saturday afternoon at the mall, followed by a good home-cooked meal and a nice long bath before bed.

And that, I'm pleased to say, is exactly what I got.

Turn the page for a sneak peek at
Akiko's next adventure!

Excerpt copyright © 2006 by Mark Crilley.
Published by Delacorte Press, an imprint of Random House Children's Books,
a division of Random House, Inc.

Chapter 1

My name is Akiko. You know how whenever something really amazing happens to you, you just can't wait to tell all your friends about it? And how sometimes the amazing thing that happened to you is so incredible and mind-blowing that even after you've told your friends about it they think you made the whole thing up? And how sometimes you don't even *dare* to tell any of your friends about the amazing thing that happened to you because it all took place while you were on another planet in a distant galaxy, surrounded by aliens and robots and exploding volcanoes and stuff, and if you were foolhardy enough to even *begin* to tell your friends a *word* of it, they would decide then and there that you were completely and irreversibly out of your mind?

Don't you hate that?

Well, hey, right now I don't care whether people who read this think I'm making it up. If they think I'm a few cards short of a full deck, they can go right ahead and think that. My only concern is to put all this stuff down on paper, in the exact order it happened, and to get the details right. Because if I don't write it down and I end up forgetting some of it after a while, that really *will* make me crazy.

Here's what you need to know:

1. I'm an ordinary sixth grader. A human being, I swear.

2. A few years back I became friends with a bunch of space people from a planet called Smoo.

3. Since then, every few months or so, these friends of mine come to Earth and say they need to take me into outer space because . . . well, they've always got one excuse or another, and it always sounds pretty reasonable at the time.

All right. Now I can tell the story.

When it comes to meeting up with me on Earth, my friends from Smoo have made some pretty weird entrances over the years: appearing in rocket ships disguised as police cars, intergalactic transit systems on shopping mall rooftops, you name it. But the way they showed up this last time really raised the bar in terms of sheer ridiculousness.

I was on vacation with my mom and dad. We were staying at my aunt Lucille's house in Minnesota. (Aunt Lucille, who has an unexplainable fondness for big floppy hats and bright orange lipstick, has made some pretty weird entrances of her own over the years, but that's a different story.) We'd been there for a couple of days, and my cousin Earl had grabbed his fishing poles and taken me down to Wacahoota Creek to see if we could catch anything "big enough to stick in the bathtub and scare the bejeezies outta Mom." Me, I wasn't sure I wanted to see Aunt Lucille any more freaked out than she already was on a day-to-day basis. But hey, it was my third day in the backwoods of Minnesota, and my entertainment options—even my reasons for staying awake—were severely limited.

So there I was with Cousin Earl, sitting at the end of a mossy makeshift dock with a fishing pole in my hands, staring down into the brown-black waters of Wacahoota Creek. In spite of Earl's claim that this spot was "world famous" as the best fishing hole in Putnam County, we'd caught nothing but dead leaves and, in what was possibly the low point of the vacation so far, a pair of discarded diapers from somewhere upstream.

"That reminds me of a funny story," Earl said, tossing the diapers as far as he could back upstream (thereby all but guaranteeing that we would catch them again a few minutes later). "This one's a real gut buster."

He went to his tackle box and began noisily rummaging through it. "You know what a gut buster is, right?" Earl had an amazing ability to tell "funny stories" that weren't funny and—this takes talent—really weren't even stories. They started at point A, moved on to point G, and then just sort of petered out somewhere in the middle of an entirely different alphabet.

Without waiting for me to either confirm or deny that I knew what a gut buster was, Earl launched into his diaper-related tale. I stopped listening by around the third rambling sentence.

Then, to my shock, I actually felt something tugging on my line.

"Hey, Earl . . . ," I said, then nearly bit my tongue off trying to stop myself midsentence. There, about six inches below the surface of Wacahoota Creek, was a small glass dome, the kind you would see at the top of a deep-sea submersible on the Discovery Channel. Through the dome, which was attached to a submarine-like vessel, I saw the face of none other than Spuckler Boach, grinning from ear to ear and giving me an enthusiastic thumbs-up. Behind Spuckler, squeezing in to make sure I'd see him, was a cheerful but panicky-looking Mr. Beeba.

I blinked in disbelief: my friends from Smoo had somehow found their way into the best fishing hole in Putnam County and were inches from rising to the surface and scaring the bejeezies out of my cousin Earl.

I motioned furiously to Spuckler and Mr. Beeba to stay underwater.

"What's up?" said Earl, still rummaging through his tackle box. "Getting crawdad nibbles again?"

"No!" I said a little too loudly, setting my fishing pole on the edge of the dock. "I mean, um . . ." I tried desperately to come up with a good reason for having said "Hey, Earl" two seconds earlier, one that wouldn't encourage him to come back over. The interstellar submarine had not broken the surface of Wacahoota Creek, but if Earl joined me on my side of the dock, he'd see it as plainly as I did. "Could, could, could you go back and repeat that last part of the story? It was, uh, so funny I gotta hear it again."

Earl turned his face in my direction, so pleased with my sudden appreciation of his genius for storytelling that he failed to notice I'd broken into a sweat. "Which part? The part about the bald-headed squirrel or the part about the surfer dude from Saskatoon?" I briefly marveled at the fact that these two topics had not only nothing to do with each other but also nothing whatsoever to do with diapers. "Um, both. You should be a stand-up comedian, Earl, I swear."

Earl chuckled, cleaning his glasses with the hem of his T-shirt. "You are not the first person to say that."

The second Earl turned back to his tackle box, I began motioning to Spuckler that he should steer their submarine as far as he could downstream and that I would catch up with them in—I pointed to an imaginary wristwatch and splayed all my fingers two times—twenty minutes.

Spuckler drew his eyebrows together and gave me a supremely confident *gotcha-cap'n-over-and-out* nod before leaning down to pull a lever.

GLOOSHHhhhhhh

The submarine dome bubbled forth from Wacahoota Creek, sending a spray of muddy water in all directions.

"What the—" Earl whipped around and began charging toward my side of the dock.

"An octopus!" I shouted before realizing it was the worst explanation I could possibly have concocted. Earl was just a couple of footsteps from catching sight of

Spuckler's sub. I bailed on talking my way out of the situation and instead jumped up and tackled Earl like a linebacker.

My plan—to the extent that I had any plan at all—was to send him flying backward across the dock toward the shore. Instead, I knocked him clear off the dock and into Wacahoota Creek. I watched with horror (and, okay, a certain amount of pleasure) as Earl flew headlong into the shallow end of the fishing hole. Then I spun around to see Spuckler's red and blue submarine rise all the way out of the water and hover there for several seconds. The upper half of Spuckler's head was visible through the dome, and he was clearly wrestling with the controls of the vehicle, trying to get it to do his bidding.

I turned back to Earl and watched him emerge from the creek, his dripping wet hair half concealed by a soggy diaper, which he was now wearing like a hat. "The heck you do that for?" he grumbled as he chucked the diaper into the mud and began fishing around for his glasses, without which, I then gratefully recalled, he could hardly see his hand before his face. If he'd still been wearing them, he'd have seen Spuckler's submarine floating in the air right behind me.

"Sorry, Earl," I said. "I was, uh, trying to stop you from knocking the bait off the dock." I rolled my eyes at my own pathetic excuse, then listened with amazement as Earl proceeded to take it quite seriously.

"The worms, eh?" Through the shallow water I could just make out the shape of Earl's glasses, a good ten feet away from where he was searching for them. "Well, that's understandable. Those suckers cost me five bucks." No way. He was practically *thanking* me. "So didja make the save or not?"

"Oh yeah," I said, watching as Spuckler's antigravity submarine rose another thirty or forty feet. "All worms are, uh, present and accounted for." The caster on my rod and reel whizzed as the hook at the end of my line—still securely fastened to the exterior of the sub—rose higher and higher into the sky. Finally I just let go of the fishing pole and allowed it to be carried away like a strange anchor.

The sub turned and silently hovered directly over me

and Earl, blocking out the sun for a moment and drizzling a considerable amount of creek water on both of us as it continued on its skyward path.

"What is it, raining?" Earl asked, squinting up at what must have looked to him like an incredibly thick and low-lying thundercloud.

"D-darnedest thing" was all I could manage to say as Spuckler's sub disappeared over a nearby oak tree. It was the first time in my life (and the last, I sincerely hope) that I have ever used the word *darnedest*.

Now that I felt sure that Earl's bejeezies would remain safely intact, I rolled up my pant legs, jumped into the water, and fished his glasses from the creek. "Found your specs, Earl," I said as I trotted up to the tackle box and grabbed a dry cloth. "Here, I'll clean them off for you."

"Thanks, cuz," said Earl. Now he really *was* thanking me.

Moments later Earl had squeezed as much water out of his jeans as he could and was heading back to the house—a good ten-minute walk—to change his clothes. "Now, I don't know what you saw there in the creek, cuz," he said before sloshing his way up the dirt road that had brought us here, "but you can take my word for it: it wasn't no octopus."

"You can say *that* again," I whispered to myself, then went off into the woods in search of a certain space-faring submarine.